HOW
BOYS
LEARN

HOW
BOYS
LEARN

Jeff Kirchick

atmosphere press

To Mom and Dad,

for whom my love is never fleeting.

AUTHOR'S NOTE ⎯

In the spring of 2010, I finished my senior thesis, *How Boys Learn*, at Princeton University under the tutelage of my friend, my advisor, and esteemed author Edmund White. The book was the culmination of a year of effort and the many years at Princeton I had spent on my creative writing efforts.

All of the stories in this book are edited and adapted from that senior thesis. At the time, we had no idea what to call it. The inspiration from each story came from some facet of my everyday life, and I wanted to find a way to twist that little sliver of my life into an interesting story. For example, "This Is the Story That I Wrote for This Week" is loosely based on my own experience with creative writing workshops, and "A Boy's School" is loosely based on a car accident I had during my senior year of high school.

Ultimately, Edmund White suggested the title *How Boys Learn* because each story features a male protagonist who must navigate the world in a very specific and uncertain way. You will also find in these stories that there is another theme about the importance of the journey versus the outcome. We learn more through our experience, even if the outcomes we desire are not there.

My dream when I graduated college back in 2010 was to ultimately become a writer/screenwriter. I never really took the risk to do that and went into tech sales instead, and I wrote my first book a few years ago, titled *Authentic Selling: How to Use the Principles of Sales in Everyday Life*. The book got good reviews and won some awards, but I figure now is the time to start taking the risk of pursuing my real dream.

I share these stories with you, the reader, as my first published work of fiction. I hope you enjoy reading them as much as I enjoyed writing them.

TABLE OF CONTENTS —

THE BOY WHO
ALWAYS CRIED
—

Entry #23:

I was called in today to look at a peculiar boy. They call him the "crying boy." Yes, that much is clear. He's two weeks old, and he has been crying ever since he left the womb. Isn't that something? That's what I thought to myself. Even when the child cries himself to sleep, we noticed during our overnight observation that you can see the faint traces of wet tears emanating from his closed eyes. They've been curious about this for some time, and obviously, the parents are very concerned. Rightfully so. I've never seen anything quite like this.

3/24/2012

Entry #24:

I went in to see that boy again. His name is Alex. A common name, but an uncommon child, to be sure. Apparently, X-rays were administered last week. No abnormalities in the body. The boy shouldn't be in any pain. But he still cries. Yes, I assure you he cries constantly. I'm no ophthalmologist, but you'd think there can only be so many tears a young boy can cry. Actually, it's funny I mention that: the ophthalmologist is my friend and colleague Dr. Adams. He was in and out the past two days when I saw the boy, flustered as all hell, probably jealous that they finally brought me in. Ironically, it was one of my grad students who suggested to me outside in the hallway that we measure the hormone levels. We did just that: low serotonin levels, low dopamine levels, and we even did some neuroimaging that revealed a smaller than average hippocampus and a potential abnormality in the nucleus accumbens. All biological explanations. The perpetual crying was still bizarre and unheard of, and I know the aforementioned student wants to study it. We administered hormone therapy and told the parents to wait this one out. Problem solved. His mother was very beautiful when she smiled at me and gave me a hug. She was very fit herself, perhaps a reasonable explanation for her extreme concern.

Daisy and I watched a movie tonight at home. It's the first time we've done something like that in a while. Naturally, she blames me for being focused on everything else but her. We're really making an effort.

And, of course, Todd is gearing up for graduation, waiting to hear back from medical school. Not much luck right now, but it will be fixed. Dalton just got a new job in Korea. It is an exciting time for the family! I haven't felt so optimistic in a long time. Children are rewarding in so many ways.

3/27/2012

Entry #26:

For the past few days, I have allowed myself to place my professional life a little more in the background. It returns to the forefront. Doesn't it always?

That boy continues to cry. The hormone therapy was clearly unsuccessful. They've been tinkering with him in my absence, but nothing. It's too bad; he is an awfully cute little baby, and the parents are tragically worried. I'd like to hate the father for the sexy wife he has, but he is just so utterly likable and nice and gentle, even in such a stressful time.

They have not once yelled at us.

Dr. Wilkinson pulled me over to chat after I did a brief observation. He told me that they had called me in because of my postpartum-depression research. Wasn't that evident?

Well, I suppose it should've been, but I don't think I deserved the attitude. It's only been a couple of years now since I won the award for developing the theory of postpartum depression occurring in children. I still had to review the statistics, the case studies, the images, etc. It was not clear-cut whether this boy Alex was a candidate, but he met several criteria nonetheless.

I felt uncomfortable making that the diagnosis, but I really had no other explanation. I made that my formal recommendation. They've proceeded accordingly. He should recover in a few months. But it is still extremely bizarre to have seen a case like this. I had to write about it.

4/20/2012

Entry #30:

Todd will be attending Columbia Medical School in the fall! Those conversations with Dean Kellerman paid dividends. I need to remember to send him something nice soon, so I am writing this down so I will not forget. I need to uphold my end of the bargain.

5/05/2012

Entry #32:

It's a good thing I read this thing even when I am not writing so much. I reminded myself to send Dean Kellerman a gift. My old self was able to use the computer and find a way to send vacation vouchers. Whenever he is able to take time, I hope he will enjoy a week-long trip to Europe.

It is a good feeling to give to others. If someone gave me such a gift, I would be thrilled. So, knowing I would be thrilled makes me imagine he might be thrilled as well. And that's quite a good feeling!

Daisy said it was a little bit too much, but then again, she just loves to argue. She just wants to stir the pot. When so many good things are going on, I don't understand why she wants to stay so grounded. Appreciate success! Revel in it! You must provide incentives to succeed. And what incentive is there when you are constantly depressed with success? She said we could give the money to charity instead. But Todd is a hard-working boy, and he deserves this. Can't leave such a delicate matter to the crapshoot of chance.

Dalton called from Korea the other day. He was concerned about the war in the Middle East, and I think he made up some joke about entering the military. I don't think he was serious, as it is obviously below him. He's got it good with Samsung. Even if we don't see eye to eye on everything, I'm happy for him, and I'm glad he thought to call me. He has a girlfriend now. Korean girl. Never knew he had the yellow fever! Good to see the kid is just like the old man!

5/29/2012

Entry #35:

Got a phone call from the ER. That crying boy just won't go away. He had an allergic reaction to this cycle of the treatment and was brought in. The parents said the symptoms haven't been subsiding, and Dr. Wilkinson was on hand to tell me how he had been dealing with them for the past couple of months. I knew he'd been dealing with them, but I thought it was inpatient visits. Not outpatient visits. He seemed to take it out on me like it was my fault. Well, you know, Dr. Wilkinson, if you need my help, you can ask. I hate when people resent others for not going out of their way. We all lead busy lives. I am a nice guy. If you ask me for help, I will be glad to help you. I'm a doctor, not a mind-reader!

I'm sorry. I just had to get this out and write it down. It's therapeutic.

6/01/2012

Entry #36:

Todd is a Harvard graduate, just like his dad! Good to have the whole family in Boston. Good to see Dalton! He brought photos of the girlfriend. She's a looker! Makes his dad jealous. Jealous and proud. Just like how I felt about the crying Alex's dad. He was pretty distraught, and for some reason, I got a guilty pleasure out of seeing it. But I'll be honest: it bothers me that I got that guilty pleasure. I know there is something wrong with that, and now that I think of it, maybe I should make an appointment with Dr. Selyck so we can talk through this.

Good thing I have this journal to write in to remind me!

Me and Dalton did have a bit of a fight, but I think it will blow over. More of the usual about the guilt. When he found out about Dean Kellerman, he really lost it. I think it is just the classic case of the older brother being jealous of the younger.

Daisy's parents were in town, too. They were acting strange. I think she told them what's going on with us. I'd like to dig further, but I probably shouldn't. Perhaps more fodder for Dr. Selyck.

7/01/2012

Entry #50:

I've taken a keen interest in the Alex boy I mentioned. Seeing him every day for the past three weeks has taken a toll on me. He literally cries non-stop. He is a rare opportunity for medical advancement. It is altogether obvious after his allergic reaction that we do not have a treatment for him if he is, in fact, suffering from postpartum depression. But the data suggests the postpartum depression is unlikely anyhow. That has taken a load off of my shoulders, even if it means I was wrong. I can't tell you how many demands were being made on me by Dr. Wilkinson, the boy's family, and even members of the media who have caught wind of this. It's really a bittersweet feeling. It's bad because I obviously want him to be cured, but it's good because of all the attention on me.

I've been seeing Dr. Selyck about these guilty, bittersweet feelings of mine. He says they are natural. He says that all people suffer from this kind of feeling during their lives. It is truly an aspect of human nature, he said. Imagine that! And people believe in God!

Alex's parents are becoming frustrated with the situation, and they are taking it out on me. I suppose I should introduce them to you. The lucky father is Matthias; his gorgeous wife is Anne. But I only speak of her beauty in the purest of ways. She reminds me of a younger Daisy but more docile, passive, friendlier. It's nice.

Anyway, Matthias and Anne are understandably upset, and I say "understandably" because I think it reflects on my ability to put myself in their shoes and relate to them in an empathetic way. I actually care for them now, so I pore over and think about this whole situation day and night. Daisy has been getting upset about it, saying I do not spend enough time at home trying to fix things with her or that I am acting uninterested in her because I bring my work home. She has even started to question my fidelity. I do not know how much longer this can go on. I'm too scared to really bring it up with Dr. Selyck, so I'm just telling you instead.

7/15/2012

Entry #52:

I'm sorry for neglecting you, dear journal, but as you know, I have been tremendously stressed. I feel like I am being tugged in so many different directions. I don't know how much longer this can go on. I can't handle it! I had to let you know.

7/16/2012

Entry #53:

Sorry for yelling at you yesterday. These religious fanatics have been lining up outside the hospital, saying that the child is some kind of anti-Christ. And then there is this other group I've heard about saying that he is an omen for some apocalyptical event, and another saying he is a reincarnated baby Jesus. This is what I hear. I don't pay attention much, but people are nuts. This whole thing is becoming very frustrating. I observe; he cries. He sleeps; he still cries. I try everything I've already tried over again. Nothing. I show him a teddy bear. He cries. Daisy tugs at me because when I am at home, I am busy figuring out a way to make the baby stop crying. Or at least understand why the fucking thing keeps crying! It's not my fault! I hope you at least believe me.

8/23/2012

Entry #54:

Daisy has been sleeping with another man. That's all I want to say about it. Oh, and we are getting divorced. And apparently, it's all my fault. That's why I haven't written in a while. I can't write anymore. Apparently, I focus too much on my work. And the stubborn brat of a child has been sent home as a national news headline. Are you happy?

8/31/2012

Entry #55:

I feel bad neglecting you. I just want you to know that I am going through the most indescribable pain right now.

I will say this, though. It would be one thing if things just came to an end. All good things come to an end, no? I'd be upset, but we would get by. This infidelity adds a whole new wrinkle. I feel so inadequate and hated. My only hope is that Todd and Dalton recognize their mother as the insufferable bitch that she is. I have done everything for them. They'd be dumb and naïve not to see it that way. I made all the money. Surely you agree. You've been such a good companion. I want you to know that.

9/28/2012

Entry #65:

Todd is in the midst of medical school. Oh, how I remember those days! I'd give anything to go back to then. Wouldn't we all?

The best news of all, though: Dalton has been promoted! Already! Success runs in this family!

They are each being so supportive of me during this difficult time. They must get that from their father. Even Dalton seemed concerned for me and asked me if I was seeing a therapist. Obviously, I told him I am not.

Things have been pretty mundane at the hospital. I've been continuing a little research on the cognitive functionality of infants. It is so hard to obtain parental consent these days. They think some of us doctors are scam artists or something. We're doctors! We're the furthest from that! People these days, huh.

I also made a visit to the Hersch family. Oh—I've forgotten to tell you. This is the family with the crying boy. He's been lost amongst the other muck I've written about, the broken-leg story, the divorce, or what have you. But yes, it seems the boy Alex is starting to temper the crying. It's still very much a problem, and they understand they will have an impaired child or at least a child who learns at a much slower rate, even if this gets resolved. But they are happy over the smallest things. I am extremely jealous to not have that ability. It is the big moments I like. You know this because I record them! But it is good to recognize one's own faults! I comfort myself knowing that.

The war is terrible, too. The soldiers are in my prayers. Crazy to think that that all just seems to be in the background, somewhere far, far away.

10/28/2013

Entry #111:

Dalton is getting married! The announcement comes a day after the Red Sox have won the World Series! Despite this, I find myself sad and depressed. And a little angry with myself for feeling that way.

6/1/2014

Entry #134:

Crazy to think that Todd is halfway through medical school. I could use him for the Hersch family. They seem to always creep back into my life. It's fine with me that they've been referred to other doctors because they can't do anything about it either. They went to the best first, and there was nothing I could do. The condition has not improved. They want me to get involved again, privately. They're willing to take enormous risks, they say. I don't know what that means. It's not like there is some kind of risky surgery that solves the problem. I still don't even know the root of the problem.

I must say, Anne gets more beautiful with age. It's been almost half a year since I have seen her. I must also confess that I continue to fantasize about her. I do not know if this is because she's objectively desirable or because I have power over her.

With that said, I had to explain to them again that there was nothing I could do. Family must be stressed out, trying to keep the media out of their house. I wonder if they even love the child anymore. I know that sounds pretty crass, but really, it is such a burden to them. How can they function? My point is that it hurt to tell Anne this. We got in an argument over it. I found the whole thing futile, and that boy has drained me.

Daisy called again to tell me how unhappy she is. Karma has served her right. Am I a bad person because hearing this actually made me happy and a little less alone? But I am unhappy too. I just can't stand to tell her that.

8/1/2014
Entry #142:

I have made vast improvements with the help of Dr. Selyck. He has me thinking not about myself so much. He says it is human nature to be selfish but that we must strive to break from that and help others. It is a hard concept, he says, but he told me an amazing thing: he gives half his income to charity! I don't know if I believe it, though. Either way, he's not married and has no kids, so easy for him to say! And he's not particularly good-looking either, so he has got to do something to feel good about himself.

8/2/2014
Entry #143:

I called Daisy today. I suppose certain feelings are fleeting. She seemed distant. I think she must be with another man. It hurts, but I try to take Dr. Selyck's advice.

9/1/2015

Entry #200:

Entry #200, you are the worst. I wanted to see what life was like a year ago, and this recollection shook me to the core. I cannot stop thinking about the Hersch family. That is all I have to say.

9/15/2015

Entry #202:

Dr. Wilkinson informs me that that crying boy (remember him?) has begun to speak, but only when he feels like it. For example, you can ask him, well, I should call him Alex.

You can ask Alex a question, and he may choose to answer it or not answer it by shaking or nodding his head, all in between sobs. It is as if he has understood language all along. Dr. Wilkinson says that he has been taken to experts all over the world (that rich Matthias not only has a hot wife but a lot of money—so that explains it!) but to no avail. Alex is a pre-schooler now and, therefore, well out of my range of expertise. Interestingly enough though, he seems to be in the pre-operational stages of cognitive functionality, right where he should be. It's just the crying. I have to record everything I know about this because it strikes me as the most interesting yet saddest story I have ever heard.

12/31/2015

Entry #210:

Dalton's wedding was yesterday. I met his wife for the second time now. She really is a beauty! They will be very happy together. It was a pleasure to meet the family. I was surprised to see how great their English is. Korea really must be a great country. It is just so rewarding to see Dalton so happy.

Todd was on break from school and was able to make it. Good to hear his war stories. Reminds me of me in my prime. He is almost done. He will be continuing at Columbia for the residency program. Didn't have to pull any strings this time.

The news is not all good. I saw Daisy at the wedding for the first time in a year. As you know, the news about the wedding was mostly good, but I knew I would have to see her again. It was not as bad as I thought. And she is not with another man, after all. She just insists that things were not going to work out. I've come to accept it by now. But something about it still made me so sad. I think I know what it feels like to be Anne and Mathias now, seeing the shell of a person but none of the potential within.

Well, Happy New Year.

1/15/2016

Entry #212:

Am I Anne Frank or Emily Dickinson?

1/31/2016

Entry #214:

As the war intensifies, the president calls for more troops, and my condition deteriorates. What condition, you ask? The human condition.

Dalton and I got into a big argument today. He is very serious about entering the military. I do not understand why. I thought our arguments about politics were just politics and that his jokes were just jokes. He is making a lot of money where he is, and he has a beautiful wife. What more can he want? I can only hope he is not so serious. I have not brought it up with Daisy because we have enough on our plates as is.

Todd is struggling as he nears completion of medical school.

But I assume he will pull it together. It will work itself out one way or another.

The Hersch family calls and wants me to start focusing my research on Alex again. They have run out of ideas. Kid is almost four years old now. The sentimental part of me knows I have to do this. I told them I need time, what with all the things going on. It was a good compromise. They were very gracious. I look forward to seeing Anne.

2/05/2016

Entry #215:

I tried calling Dalton every day for the past week. No response. I hope that our argument was not that serious. It seems like we are winning the war; it should be over soon. So, I hope that he takes that into account.

2/28/2016

Entry #220:

I called Dalton and finally got an answer from his wife, Grace. I could not believe what she told me. She said Dalton will not speak with me and that he does not want to end up like me. She seems upset as well. I can only take this in stride for now. Dr. Selyck is helping, but he's also really pissing me off. He's suggesting I played a big part in all of this. Weird strategy for a therapist to make you feel bad so you can feel better. I might need to fire him.

5/20/2016

Entry #250:

Todd graduated from medical school. Seems like yesterday I was writing about him graduating from college. The family was in town again. I cannot begin to describe how proud I am. He says he wants to help out with Alex now. Daisy made it. I must say I still think she is beautiful even after everything. I told her there is always a place for her in the house.

6/26/2016

Entry #257:

I started my visits to the Hersch family today. Haven't seen Alex in ages. But yes, he still cries. Haven't I known this all along? Yes, but I've neglected you, dear journal. I try not to tell you that I hear about him on the news. That people speculate about him. That my name is mentioned alongside his. It saddens me, so I tell you about all the other things instead. And yet here I am.

The most amazing thing happened today, however. His parents put me in a room with him and told me to do whatever it is that I do. I honestly had no plan. The boy saw me and sobbed. He is a far cry (no pun intended) from the boy I knew years ago. He is a handsome young boy.

Guess what happened? He stopped crying. He dried his eyes and looked at me. Now, I knew I had heard that he could temper the crying. But I wasn't expecting this sudden change. I went to open the door to show his parents, and he immediately began crying again. When I sat down, he stopped. When I went to the door, he cried. This continued until I eventually sat down.

I tried to ask him a few questions, but nothing. Eventually, he began crying again. I took a few notes and left.

7/01/2016

Entry #261:

Amazing news!

I got a letter from Dalton today. No return address. It says he is sorry about our fight but that he will be ready to talk to me soon. I cannot believe this news! This whole thing with him has been haunting me. Wait until I tell Dr. Selyck, ha!

I went to see Daisy to tell her, and she was so happy to see me. I think maybe we have a shot. We'll see.

The Parkers invited me over for dinner. What great neighbors I have. They inquired about Daisy, and I told them what faith I have right now. I regret the times I told Daisy they were just hustlers. They're nice people.

Even the war seems to be coming to an end. I think it is time we stop meddling in the affairs of others and put America first. I think we've learned from this war.

Time to go see Alex.

7/02/2016

Entry #262:

What an odd day. I sat down with Alex. He asked me a question. "Why did you tell my parents I stopped crying?" I hope you can try to imagine the shock of hearing the boy speak. To my knowledge, he had only nodded his head before. I told him I thought I had to. He did not answer any more of my questions, and I decided I could not say a word about this encounter.

7/03/2016

Entry #263:

I went to see Alex again, and he continued to cry. I asked him if he could stop crying so we could have a chat like the time before. He did not answer. Then I asked, do you choose to cry or is it out of your control? He did not answer. So, I asked, do you choose to cry? He nodded his head "yes." He chooses to cry. I asked, have you chosen to cry all along? He nodded "yes." Bullshit, I think to myself. Kid has some neurological malfunction we don't know about yet. So, I ask him, do you remember me from years before? He nodded "yes." So, I cleverly thought to myself how to prove this brat wrong. I even phrased it well. I said, "If you are so clever, tell me the biggest difference between me when you were born and me now?" He stopped crying and said, quite nonchalantly, in fact, that I wear glasses now. What is there to make of this?

To me, the fascinating thing about this is his language acquisition. His ability to comprehend very important things at so young an age. Indeed, Dr. Wilkinson noted this. Yet the boy refuses to take tests for us. It makes things rather difficult. It's as if he knows what is going on.

8/22/2016

Entry #265:

Dalton went off to fight in the war. That is why I have not been hearing from him. That is why I got a letter with no return address. I only know this because Grace called me on a whim to tell me. I lost my shit with her. I can't even write about this right now.

10/31/2016

Entry #266:

I know it's been a while. I've been too scared to come back here and deal with the reality of how shitty I am. As I prepare to hand out Halloween candy to little kids, I cannot stop thinking about children. Children, almost like Dalton, wherever he is. And I cannot stop thinking about you, dear journal. You are my only real friend in this world.

2/02/2017

Entry #268:

Alex and I have become friends, I think. We have had real conversations. He is a brilliant boy, the things he understands. I tell no one about our conversations because I am wary of his intelligence. I only record it here.

2/15/2017

Entry #269:

When I think about Dalton, I think about my selfishness. It was my selfishness that didn't want him to do what he wanted to do for himself. It was always this way, wasn't it? I cannot describe the feeling of not being on speaking terms with your own son, but then knowing everything will be okay, and then finding out that he is in some foreign land before you can even shake his hand and both move on. It is the worst feeling in the world.

The good news to report is that Todd is doing very well. He relies less and less on me with each passing day, and he comes to visit his mother every few weekends, too. Todd is a good kid, and he's been keeping tabs on both of us for the last several months. To be honest, I am not sure where I would be without him. I sit in this big empty house, thinking about my failures as a husband, father, and doctor, too scared to write in this thing for fear of reminding myself how horrible I am.

2/28/2017

Entry #271:

My findings lead me to trust that Alex has been consciously crying for a long time. Perhaps even since birth. He remembers the minute details of being a newborn baby. These are details no human being has ever been able to recall. How do I know he knows them well? Because I remember those days so vividly. They were the best of times. I just didn't know it then.

3/01/2017

Entry #272:

Today, I was sitting down with Alex, and he asked me why I do not cry with him.

3/02/2017

Entry #273:

I have begun coming to the Hersch family during the day when Matthias is not around. Anne always makes me a glass of lemonade. She is a true sweetheart, and she continues to grow prettier with age. She really understands what I am battling through at the moment.

I asked Alex again why he does not cry around me. He doesn't answer. He stares out the window. I then asked if he could do me a favor and stop crying around his parents. He told me that would be impossible.

3/02/2017

Entry #274:

If Alex chooses to cry, there must be a way to make him stop. I've told Dr. Wilkinson that this is a theory of mine (but I did not dare tell him why), and we've brought Dr. Alexander in for his expertise in neuro, but Alex resists all testing as if trying to prevent us from learning. I have built a trust with Alex, and I cannot tell anyone about my findings with him. I have learned through betraying him how quickly he understands when I have done so, and I even felt a little guilty telling Dr. Wilkinson my theory. I just want to help Alex. I feel like he is my only shot right now. For redemption, or some of it, I guess.

Entry #276:

I have done a terrible, terrible thing.

Entry #277:

I have been so ashamed to tell you this. I have taken advantage of Anne. This happened almost two months ago. It was during one of my daytime visits. We were having a heart-to-heart conversation. She broke down crying. I told her, what if I had a cure for him? She was already gripping me tightly. I had whispered it in her ear. Oh, how hopeful she looked. How beautiful. She deserves that great man for a husband, not scum like me after what I have done. She was so hopeful, and then the little devil in me re-emerged and started caressing her and taking advantage of her sadness and asked her what the price was going to be. Soon she was on her knees playing with my cock, and I know it only felt good because of the sick fetish I have had for her since the beginning. Sick! I am sick! I took advantage of a beautiful woman, knowing that she would never be able to tell anyone. And I have no cure for her son, my friend, who consciously cries all the time, who is some sort of rare genius, who disallows me from telling any single person any of these details because if I lose his trust, I will lose any hope of furthering my research.

I have seen Anne, and I have seen Daisy over the course of the past two months, and when I see either of them, I cannot stand to live with myself anymore. Success is nothing compared to happiness, and happy I am not.

I owe it to the Hersch family to find a cure for their son. I am afraid to consult any of my colleagues, but I will have to try somehow.

6/12/2017

Entry #278:

Todd called today to find out what is wrong. I hung up the phone after a short but untruthful explanation. He is also a reminder of how awful I am. It's too bad there is no hell for me.

Like Alex, I, too, cry myself to sleep every night. I never thought I would say this, and please don't tell anyone, but I am thinking about ending it. I think it might be best for everyone so I can stop hurting people.

6/17/2017

Entry #279:

When I look into Anne's eyes, I see the same dumb hope I saw in Dalton's. Doesn't she realize the fraud that I am? I am so awful, and I know it, and yet I cannot just admit that to her. Isn't that what she deserves? Why am I such a bad person? I cannot even bear to tell any of this to Dr. Selyck. Alas, dear journal, as we come to the end, it is just you and me. So now you know—you are the only one I have been truthful to. I can confide in you, confess to you, and I want you to know now that Daisy has told me she loves me and that as much as we can feel the pull of the sadness of our own actions, there is always hope. And there will always be hope.

22

6/22/2017

Entry #280:

Seeing Alex makes me feel guilty, but I think we are getting somewhere. He begins to open up. I asked him how he knew when I told others about him, and he said he could tell by my behavior. That is a start. He does not tell me what it is about my behavior. But I trust him, just as he trusts me.

I ask him if he thinks he might be able to stop crying. He says maybe.

Hearing that "maybe" makes me cry a little less myself.

7/03/2017

Entry #287:

It turns out the pain Alex has been experiencing lately is due to brain cancer. My guess is that this stems from whatever neurological disorder Alex has. I hesitate to say he has a disorder, however, because he has been so conscious of everything from the beginning.

Am I sad? Yes, I am. You'd think that things are relative, and this is no big deal. That's not the case. Alex is like my Dalton. And yet, I have become numb to the pain. I no longer cry.

7/10/2017

Entry #289:

As Alex enters the hospital, he continues crying all the time, just as he did when he was born. He no longer talks to me. Even when we are alone, I am no longer acknowledged. The connection is lost. I can only hope he will recover.

Daisy has moved in with me. As connections are severed, others are re-gained. We are in this together. I have begun explaining my research to her, the Hersch family, and my colleagues. As Alex sits alone in a hospital bed, there is no way for him to know that I have betrayed him. I can only hope he understands that I have betrayed him for his own sake. People look at me as some kind of hero, but I do not need or deserve the acclaim. In fact, it makes me feel worse about betraying Alex. But as I said, we can only have hope, and my hope is that Alex would understand.

I love him.

7/15/2017

Entry #292:

I have declined all interviews with national news outlets as Alex cries incessantly. He is going to die.

7/15/2017

Entry #293:

You know what, though? These people are sick. They show up to schools to talk to victims minutes after a school shooting, and they try to shove microphones in your face when you are trying to cure a dying child. For what? Ratings? Money?

7/16/2017

Entry #294:

I sat by Alex's bedside today and tried to talk to him alone. I told him all kinds of things. I tried to ask questions. He cried.

Then, I told him I did not want him to die. I told him that he reminded me of Dalton. That he was brave. That he was like a son to me. And that I loved him. Can you believe an asshole like me had these feelings? The same asshole who cannot look Alex's mother in the face? I cannot even know what she thinks of me. She probably pities me, and herself. She probably has no energy to hate me anymore.

But Alex stopped crying when I said these things. Even his trust in me makes me feel filthy. But yes, I had the selfish pleasure of seeing him stop crying. He squeezed my hand.

7/18/2017

Entry #295:

Alex died last night in his sleep. Ironically, when he slept, he would never cry. And he was not crying when he died.

I did not cry when I heard the news. I was braced for this. I hugged Matthias and Anne. I also spoke to Anne privately. I told her how sorry I was. She said it was okay. But I re-emphasized how sorry I was, hoping she would understand. Again, she said it was okay. I have failed to redeem myself to her, and for that, I am truly worthless. Just as she cannot explain things fully to Matthias, I cannot explain myself fully to Daisy, and for that, we will struggle. My one hope was that I could speak to Anne, but I don't deserve the consolation. I deserve the worst imaginable punishment.

9/05/2017

Entry #296:

It is nice being with Daisy again. We are happy now that we have each placed things in perspective. We share the same pains, but we also share the same memories of happiness.

Todd continues to do well, too, and it sounds like he has a serious girlfriend. I'm happy for him.

The Hersch family came over for dinner last week, which inspired me to write again. Anne and I share a secret that can never be told, but surprisingly, she does not act with any malice toward me. She acts as if she loves me the way that we should love anyone else. She forgives me, I think, because she understands.

The Hersch family, my colleagues, and the media—even

25

Daisy—they are all curious to know what it was that gripped Alex. Indeed, my research, my many hours playing with Alex alone when no one could see him snapping out of his crying, the conversations we had, the friendship we formed, this was all a big shock to people who had only known him as a crying boy. Everyone wants to know my professional opinion on the matter.

To the public, I have said that this was a neurological disorder. The public also does not know all the facts. It is believable to them.

To my colleagues, I have explained that he had a highly functional brain that advanced at a rapid rate, like a young genius, except faster. I then went on to discuss the small size of his hippocampus and nucleus accumbens as well as the bizarre firing I noticed in Alex's amygdala the one time I was able to hook him up to an fMRI.

To Daisy, I say quite simply that I do not know what was wrong with Alex, but that is not true at all.

What is true is what I told the Hersch family outside on my driveway last week, out in the darkness, as Daisy was doing the dishes. They hadn't asked what was wrong, but I had to tell them because they had suffered for so many years. They are good people, and they deserved to know. And I thought knowing it might make them feel better: it was, I thought, a small, good thing to tell them, so I did. I told them that there was nothing wrong with Alex. There was nothing wrong with him.

THE BRIGHT LIGHTS   —

I'm fuckin' thirsty.

Weigh-in is still two days away, and my throat already feels like sandpaper. When I try to swallow, I can't. There's nothing, and mid-swallow, I just start gagging. The noise interrupts my class, which I can't pay attention to anyway. A couple people turn their heads to look at me buried in my sweatshirt. I don't know if they feel sorry for me, but I do know what they're thinking: *he's a wrestler.*

I don't know if it's the hunger or the thirst that kills me more. It's the hunger at first, at the beginning of the week when the weigh-in looms in the distance. I look around the cafeteria, see everyone eating, and wonder if just a bite of something will be okay, but I know at this point it's just discipline, discipline, discipline. I keep repeating it in my head. I sit down with the wrestlers with a salad and don't talk much, just hating myself.

You're not supposed to cut your water at first. That's why the thirst creeps in slowly, right before the match, the practice before when all we do is sweat, sweat, sweat. But I have to start early. When you're a 135 and you're listed at 167 during football season ... no, that's not a good way of putting it; everyone starts out big and cuts down. I'll say it like this. When you're a 135 the morning of weigh-in and 152 the next day, you know you're gonna have to cut your water early for the next match. Unless you wanna lose it all at once, really just drain everything out of yourself the night before and risk dehydration. I don't know why I put myself through it, but doing it gradually like that just makes me feel better.

That's what I think about as the bell rings and my class finally ends. How this is the norm in western Pennsylvania, or as we call it, PA. This is life in PA. There is no room for complaining. You wake up, you go to work, you come home, and you sleep. You make a living. My family lives modestly, just like everyone else does here. My father works in the steel mill, just like the fathers of most of my best friends. I imagine I'll work there one day, too, once I'm done with school, but I'm only a junior, and Pitt-Johnstown has been sending me letters about wrestling in college, and my dad wants me to be the first member of our family to make it to college. I think it's just because he doesn't want me to give up wrestling.

* * *

All these years later, you would think I would end up the same as him, but no, Doctor, I don't work in the steel mill like my dad did. I own a construction company, actually, and I've done real well with it. It doesn't mean that I'm no longer attached to the community, because I am. I still go to all the Shaler Area home matches, the state tournament, everything. I know who the studs are and all that shit from the newspaper or word of mouth in the stands. I know half of it is because my kid is on the team, but I also know that a lot of it has to do with me never wanting to let it go. Even my wife gets a little grumpy every now and then when I talk about it; I bet you know what that's like. My "glory days," she calls it, says they're long gone. I know it's true, but you never really let it go. And that's why it's so difficult to see my kid struggling right now.

* * *

We're wrestling North Alleghany this weekend. It's the biggest match of the year because we're both undefeated and a loss could mess up the perfect season. But it's my biggest match ever because I have to wrestle Stetter. He's their captain and the returning state champ at 135. Last year, I qualified for States, which is a big deal in PA, but I didn't even place. Stetter is a senior. I'm only a junior. He already committed to Penn State, and me, I'll be lucky to get another letter from Johnstown.

I've only really heard about him. I didn't stay long enough at States last year to really watch him. But I saw him. He was a scary-looking guy. I thought to myself, "Boy, I'm glad I don't ever have to face that guy." I was a 140-pounder then, and guys like Stetter, they never miss weight and move up a weight class 'cause they're too tough. He had a bunch of tattoos. I remember I saw him in this one match at States, and he had this huge dragon tattoo on his back. I was thinking how badass it was, and before I knew it, the match was over. Stetter had pinned the guy in thirteen seconds.

I've been trying not to think about it, but everyone keeps reminding me. "Hey, man, you're gonna kill Stetter this weekend," or, "You're his first real test this year." It's constant, in the locker room, outside of class, or from guys who aren't even on the team because somehow the whole school seems to know about the match and how I drew their big horse. I know I'm rising in the ranks in PA now; the expectation is I'll place, and I know all eyes will be on me, whether you're a Shaler guy or an NA guy. But I don't feel like I have a shot. Stetter has never lost a match in PA in his life. He's gunning to be one of six four-time state champs in PA history.

* * *

The more I think about it, the less trivial it seemed back then. It was supposed to be one of those things that really mattered at the time and made you scared shitless, but then you looked back several years later and laughed, but deep down, you still really cared. I guess I can laugh about it sometimes, but it doesn't change that it was the single most vivid memory I've ever had and that, somehow, it had *changed* me. I'm frustrated. I can't quite explain it to you because you're an outsider; you wouldn't really understand what I went through.

*   *   *

It's the self-loathing. I feel it now as I get in bed. Tomorrow is Friday, the day before the big match on Saturday night. It's not quite Hell Day. It will be brutal, I know it, but it will really get awful Friday night. But there's this feeling I get as I get in bed that I just hate myself. I feel bad for myself, sucked out completely, unable to think straight.

It's putting myself through this daily grind. I don't get what it is about being locked in this steaming room doing the most strenuous physical labor in the thick of winter. It's just depressing. There's no way around it. I know I'll still be sweating once I put on my jacket and step out into the frigid air, and I'll be scraped up, but I'll just be drained and feeling like shit. I'll feel worthless. It's like asking yourself every day why you put yourself through hell, and then you sort of know the answer, but no one ever really tells it to you straight, and then you get out into the cold and you feel alone. And that's the feeling I get as I crawl into bed.

I think some of it has to do with dinner. Because my mom had poured me a glass of water, and I told myself I'd allow half a pound for hydration, and the glass is a full pound. But once it hit my lips, I just couldn't put it down. I just chugged the whole thing just like that in front of my dad, who gave me this look. You know the kind of look I'm talking about, this disappointed one but hidden from my mom, it lasted so short. He just kept eating his dinner, and then it sunk in as I looked down at my plate—and it was a small portion because of my upcoming match—that I would have nothing to drink with it. I thought to myself whether I wanted to deal with my hunger and end up being even thirstier than I was or just not eat dinner and be content with only having to lose the extra pound.

I chose to take a few bites, but I could barely chew; I had none of those juices in my mouth, really, and I wanted to break down and cry in front of my parents, but I knew what my dad would do. I excused myself and went to my room.

I had tried doing my homework, but I couldn't help but feel guilty. I threw a pinch of tobacco on my gums. My mouth was so dry I could barely spit. If anything, I got a few ounces of water out of me. But I was just sitting there, you know, at my desk, with the dip in my mouth, pinching it tight with my tongue against my gums, closing my eyes. It's a weird feeling, doing that and just praying it will make you take a shit. I was willing to settle for anything tonight, even a small one, just so I could make up for the extra water and maybe go eat a little something. But it wouldn't come. My body was too drained.

And then I realized that until Saturday, I would get no help from pissing or shitting. Maybe I'd piss out a few ounces before weigh-in, but that was gonna be it. The only help I'd get would be from whatever weight I would float naturally between then and Saturday. And I was still six or seven pounds over.

The thought made me gag as I tried to spit out the dip, which was too difficult because my mouth was too dry. I accidentally swallowed some of it and immediately rushed to the toilet. I threw up at first, just a little bit of liquid and the blackness of the tobacco. And then it was constant dry-heaving because there was nothing else left in me. My stomach burned with each heave until, finally, it ended. I could hear a commotion downstairs, but then I heard my dad telling my mom to shut the fuck up and let me learn a lesson.

It was then I decided to go to bed. First, I brushed my teeth and took a shower. In the shower, I was tempted to drink the water. A friend of mine had done that once but couldn't stop himself and missed weight, so I didn't dare even start, but I gave it a good couple minutes of thought just standing there. And then I thought about how every night after I won a match, my dad and I would drink beers together and laugh and not worry about making weight. But if I lost, there was none of that, not even a "nice try." So, as I lay there in bed and thought about going through hell to wrestle Stetter on Saturday, and my dad was pretending that it's just another match, but it wasn't, I just felt like crying or living another life, anywhere. They say I'm lucky to be an American, but I would trade to be anything else right now.

*   *   *

Yeah, I'd say so, that there was a sense of solitude because of my father. That's why I try to take it easier on my kid. But I don't let up completely because I haven't really made up my mind whether my father was really a bad influence. I mean, sometimes I think I owe it all to him. I wouldn't have been so committed if it weren't for him. It was through him that I learned to do it for myself, ironically. There was this breaking point I reached; it had happened well before the match with NA, where I just decided that I couldn't lose. I would still cry at night, and I would still question myself, sure. But at one point, for some reason or other, it just all seemed right. It felt like this could be the one crowning achievement where no one else would get in my way. It was the ultimate physical battle. I mean, I know they say swimming is tough, gymnastics takes a lot of skill, and football is physical ... but wrestling really combined everything, and it was one-on-one, all eyes on you, everything on you, really. And I don't know how I realized it, but I did, and it didn't make me any happier, but it made me feel like I was *going* somewhere. Like, one day, I would be standing on a podium, and this euphoric feeling would come that made everything seem *worth* it. I want my son to know that feeling.

*   *   *

I wake up after surprisingly falling asleep pretty quickly, but maybe it's because I've been so damn tired, and I realize it's still all the same. One more day of school before the match, and it will all be over. I've been hearing it all week, and though I am ragged and worn, I do feel the excitement beginning to kick in. It's the nervous energy. There will be a pep rally tonight, and though I know I'll be too tired to have any fun, it will be nice to be in the spotlight, and it will motivate me to keep going.

I walk down the stairs in my underwear and into the basement, holding myself and feeling goosebumps because of the intense cold. It's dark, but I find the light at the bottom, and at the end of the hall, there is my scale. I step on. 139.6 pounds. Perfect. I go upstairs and measure out a few ounces of orange juice and toast half a bagel. I make sure to eat the bagel first and then drink the orange juice, until I realize I haven't peed yet. I race into the bathroom and pee, but only a little bit comes out: dark yellow, almost brown. Then, somewhat warmer now, I run down into the basement and weigh myself again. 140, right on the dot, right where I want to be with over a full day to go. I'm surprised at how good I've been this week. Usually, I have six or seven pounds to cut right before the match, but right now, I have over twenty-four hours, and I am only five pounds over. Then again, I've cut my water early this time because I was irresponsible last week. I try to think to myself about what I can afford to do. I'll float off about three pounds between now and the match, and if I work real hard in practice or do some extra running on Saturday, that's another three to five pounds of sweat, even though my body won't want to sweat at all; it will go into that state of shock where sweating is real tough, but I know I can do it. So, I reckon I can afford to eat and drink two pounds worth of food and water by Saturday.

I look above the scale and see the wrestling schedule I taped to the wall at the beginning of the season. I've been marking down the wins and losses throughout my high school career, but this year, there is nothing but wins. I'm undefeated, and I'm ranked fourth in the state. Still, Stetter is the best guy

I'll ever face, the best there is, in fact. As I look at the schedule, I wonder if he is somewhere nearby doing the same exact thing. But then I think to myself, he is out there to kill me, that asshole. I'm going through hell for this shit. I punch the schedule with my fist, even though it hurts a bit.

"Fuck you, Stetter. I'm coming for you," I say to myself, suddenly energized and ready for school, feeling like I might be able to focus today.

*　*　*

It was definitely an up-and-down. Certainly, Doctor. The periods of self-loathing were followed by periods of faith, which were followed by more hatred or, in the case of a win, like you were on top of the world. In the case of a loss, you questioned yourself; you had to tell yourself that this is what was going to make you stronger. That this was God's plan. It grew your faith in Him. But it was never easy. Never. The emotional volatility, it gets to you; it's like nothing else. I'd say it's almost like being in love when you wonder what the other person is thinking, how stable you are. I'd say it's worse because at least love was permanent; you always have the person there if it works out. But the glory of winning, I thought, was always fleeting. I wasn't sure. It was always the best feeling in the world, but then you had the next match, and eventually, it would all be over anyway, and so then what? This is what I thought, for a while, at least. I didn't know, like my dad did then, that I could become immortal.

*　*　*

At school, I am thirsty again. When I look at the vending machine or the people drinking their soda, I fantasize about it. I imagine myself as them. Or I fantasize about the moment after weigh-in when I will drink all the water in the water fountain, and then after the match where I will drink endless amounts of water and eat tons of pizza before I go home and drink some beers with my dad. And then I remember I have to wrestle Stetter and that maybe I won't live my fantasies out completely. But I do dream of that time when I will binge, and then when the season ends, I will be fat and happy again. We call it "wrestling fat," where you're not really fat because you're still in better shape than most people, but you know, fat, relatively speaking.

All day, people are wishing me luck, patting me on the shoulder, telling me they'll be there. It makes me excited and makes me think less about my current pain. These are people who idolize me, my sacrifice. These are people who are proud to have me represent their school. I'm like one of their celebrities. Even the girls are saying things to me, like they don't know all too much about wrestling but they saw me at the last meet, and hey, you looked good out there, we'll see you tomorrow night. Maybe you'll come to Lucy's party afterward? "Yeah, sure," I keep saying. I think I weird them out because I talk like a zombie; I can hardly think straight. Didn't even realize there was a party, but it makes me feel even better about all of this ending soon; it could be like a huge victory party for us. I just try to play it cool with them like I am focused on one thing and girls can wait and feel lucky to even invite me. But I also know that that's really all I have the energy for anyway. Maybe it's a good thing the misery is making me distant, so they'll chase me. Or maybe it's making them think I'm an asshole. I also don't have the energy to answer that question in my head.

*   *   *

I liked this one girl back then, Carly. She was a cheerleader, so I knew she would be at all the big matches. I wondered if she actually liked the matches or just came because she had to. She had a lot of school spirit, though, so I imagine she had

35

to think I was something special. I mean, I was a good-looking kid. I know it's hard to believe because, look at me, I'm fat now. But back then, after sweating so much before the match and then ripping off everything and just wearing that singlet tight against my lean body ... I was a well-oiled machine. I mean, I was big for a 135; when I came out there, people couldn't believe I made weight. I remember one guy on an opposing team even said, "Hey, Tyler Mariotti cut off his cock to make weight today." Everyone laughed.

The joke stuck. I was always cutting off my dick to make weight.

*　*　*

Practice rolls around, and I wander into the locker room, feeling like I might not make it. There is this terrible feeling in my legs, like they can't move anymore, yet somehow, they know that they are going to be put through abuse for the next two hours, and so they are just giving up now. I'm about six over now. I figure if I can lose four pounds in practice, I can go home, have a small dinner, and only have a couple of pounds to cut the next day right before the match. But it won't be easy because I have nothing left to give. My body doesn't wanna move, and it sure as hell doesn't wanna sweat. I'm already depleted of about eight to nine pounds' worth of water that my body needs just to feel normal, and even then, I bet I'd still be pissing yellow. I put on layer after layer of t-shirts and shorts, and then sweatshirts and sweatpants. I'm about three to four layers deep when I pull the drawstrings on my sweatshirt and throw a pair of socks over my hands. The only part of my body that you can really see is my eyes.

The trick is to get the sweat going. Once you get it going, it doesn't really stop; you just need to push it into another gear and make the most of it once you get it going, but don't fuckin' lose it, or you'll put yourself through hell. I'm sitting on the mat before practice, just trying to milk the clock and hoping time will stop until I feel better, but I know it won't. Then our coach comes up, Coach Thurston. He's a small, muscly guy with lots of hair. He's got a beard. He doesn't yell a lot, only when he needs to, but he's tough as nails. He comes up and says, "Mariotti, get the fuck off your back and get your fat ass sweating. Let's go! Everyone, weight-cutting day; do what you need to do." We're not supposed to lie down.

I get up and grab my partner, Terry. Black kid, tried out for basketball two years ago but didn't make it, but has lots of natural ability in wrestling. He's my backup. He's a freshman, and he's been intimidated by me all year, but slowly, he has been starting to assert himself a bit. I still always beat him, but he knows what I'm up to now, so he wrestles me pretty close. He knows the drill. We just are going to wrestle each other for a while. Not too hard because I feel like I might die, but just hard enough that I'll start sweating, and we'll just roll around for a while 'til I get that sweat, and then I'll run with it.

*　　*　　*

There was always this feeling like you wouldn't make it through on the weight-cutting day, and I remember that time was particularly tough. I don't know why I had been so irresponsible the week before such a big match, but I definitely paid for it by the amount of weight I had to cut. I'd heard that Stetter was a big cutter too, so I didn't think I'd lose anything because of it; we'd both feel awful out there on the mat, have short wind, but boy, did I feel like I might lose it then. Sometimes, it's sort of depressing to feel like you've lost that kind of discipline. I mean, I know it's not normal; I know it's insane, fine. But it's tough to feel like you've reached the peak of your physical condition, the epitome of discipline. What if you could carry that over into other things? What if you refused to relax in your career? I think about that a lot. It's really sad. I really think this is why I have been depressed. I never feel like I am doing enough. I can't even get my own kid to see the good in it. Anyway, I don't know what it was that pushed me through those practices, and sometimes I don't even feel like me and that kid are the same person, but I sure as hell know I admire that guy for what he did. I admire my kid, too, even though I can see the struggle in his eyes, because he reminds me of myself. I'm just not quite sure how to handle it, and thinking about that whole ordeal is bringing back these memories that I haven't really ever sorted out in my mind.

* * *

It's the end of practice, and I am soaking wet. I feel like I must have exceeded my expectations, but I am still really nervous when I get to the scale. It had taken me thirty minutes to even feel moisture on my face, but as soon as I got the sweat going, I hit the treadmill until I couldn't feel my legs anymore. Then, when I felt like I had nothing left to give and that I might pass out, I grabbed Terry and made him stay after practice with me to keep drilling until I collapsed. Literally, I fell, and Terry was scared shitless. I told him I was okay and to just bring me a little bit of water, but only a little. He came right back with a few ounces. I eyed it carefully and drank it quickly, sighing and panting heavily. He helped me up, and I had him help walk me down to the locker room.

I strip naked at the scale with Terry watching. My teammates are showering, but some of them are getting dressed and peeking at me through the corner of their eyes, seeing if I'll be okay. Just before, we'd all been sitting after practice, listening to our two captains give us our final pep talk and then explain how to conduct ourselves at the upcoming pep rally. I could barely focus. I was thinking that I needed to get my sweat back, and I was wondering if I'd be able to eat or drink something at the pep rally. The one thing I did get was when one of them said something like, "You will remember this night for the rest of your lives." I fucking believed it.

137.3. I've only lost three pounds. Not even. The body plays tricks on you when it's sucked out. You feel like you just lost ten pounds, and your body says no, only 2.7 pounds; this is what you get for treating me like shit all week. Still, only 2.3 pounds to go ... if I could eat and drink about .7 and lose a pound between now and the match naturally, I'd only have to sweat off a couple more. I usually float off more weight naturally, but when you're so sucked out like I am, it doesn't work so effectively, like you want it to, like you need it to. I feel like shit knowing that I can't really reward myself, that there is still a lot of suffering ahead, but still, I can see the light at the end of the tunnel, and after a night of sleep, maybe I will feel better. I know what I'll do. I'll eat some granola bars, maybe even some candy bars. At this point, the calories don't matter; it's the size of the food. I just need the energy, the sugar, anything. I'll flood myself with bars and granola and then give myself a decent bit of water, and it will be just enough to shave off the last few pounds. And then I'll fuck Stetter up.

*   *   *

I don't know if it was really just the weight. The sport instills an element of fear in you, too. It's scary to go out there. Not even when everyone is watching, but even just when you're one-on-one, alone. It's not a fear of getting hurt, really. It's a fear of losing your dignity, or pride, or something. I can't really put my finger on it. It's scary to wonder if you'll get too tired to function, if you'll reach that pivotal moment between giving up and fighting through. No one wants to get there because giving up in a sport like that has gotta be the worst feeling in the world. But then you add on top of that that everyone is watching you, that you're alone out there with no one to lean on, that at any time you could falter or be too tired to go on and everyone is out there watching you, judging you ... that you have put so much personal sacrifice into this one six-minute frame and that you could lose and fuck it all up and then where do you go from there? Was it worth it? It's scary. There's an element of fear, but no, it wasn't just because of the weight.

* * *

The pep rally sucks. I feel like fainting. I have nothing to give. Even when Carly comes up to me and looks gorgeous with her red hair and her locks and her cheerleading uniform, and even flirts with me for once, I can only say I am excited about the match and maybe I'll see her at the party afterward, but I'm not feeling well, so who knows if I'm going? She frowns, and I feel like a jerk, but I have nothing to say, and even though I care, I don't care right now. I just want it to end, and even when they start talking about my match-up with Stetter as one of the biggest match-ups in PA all year, I am just sorta surprised because I don't think it's really that big. I mean, the kid is an animal. I don't belong in that category with him quite yet, but I do think I can beat him if everything somehow goes right.

I finally leave right after they light the bonfire. My dad pulls his pick-up around and tells me to hop in.

"I know what you feel like," he says bluntly, "so we're getting the fuck out of here. Champ needs his sleep."

Somehow, hearing him call me a champ makes everything better. I remain quiet, and as I look out the window, I know I am smiling just a little bit as the snow falls down outside because I can tell he's looking at me from time to time.

It's still snowing as I try to sleep at night, but I can't right now. It's always like this right before. I had a protein bar and half a pound of water, and by the time I got in bed, I was just three over, but I could barely talk, I was so dehydrated. I am lying in bed, just thinking. I am more tired than I have ever been in my life, but I can't fall asleep because I just want to run out of bed and run the shower and drink until I vomit. It's the weirdest feeling ever, being so tired and being so incapable of sleep. I want to punch something. I know it's getting late, and I need to wake up and make sure I sweat, and so that just adds to the frustration and makes it harder. I hate myself. I don't know why I'm putting myself through it. I guess this is going to make it all even more worth it, but enough is enough. I don't get it. I simply don't know what it is. I feel bad for me.

I'm thinking about tomorrow night, and I am twirling my hair because I am as nervous as all hell and wondering how it will go. I don't know what to expect from Stetter. He was scary. I only hear stories about him. He's broken arms and even legs. Someone told me that Stetter has no soul; he sold it away and doesn't believe in God anymore. I don't know what to think. I know I'm good, but I don't really know just how good Stetter is. Eventually, thinking about nothing but the following night, after tossing and turning and thinking and trying to be able to swallow just once, I fall asleep.

* * *

The sleepless nights were the worst, especially the times when you had to get up in the morning and keep running, and your legs already felt like Jell-O. That day was hell.

Not just because I felt like hell, but because it was hell to wait until 6 PM for a weigh-in and 7 PM for the match to start, and God knows when all of this shit will be over for me. But yes, it did affect my high-school experience because I barely slept. I was always worried, anxious, self-deprecating. I don't know how I ever slept. I don't know how I was ever social. My mood went down the chute with everything else.

* * *

When I wake up, I don't wanna talk to anybody. I get down to the basement, and as I expect, I am two over. I don't need to lose exactly two pounds, just a little less, because I'll lose a little bit naturally before the match. But if I want any sort of sustenance, I'll need to lose at least two.

I put on my sweat gear. I want to get this over with. It's only 10 AM but the sooner I am at 135, the better I'll feel. I sit in the corner of my basement and just think for a while. I wonder if my dad will take me to the sauna today. Probably not. He says it's the cheap way out. And besides, he won't wanna stay to watch me to make sure I don't pass out.

I get the jump rope. The first few skips I can't even complete, and finally, I trip and fall. I'm lying on the floor, crying. I can't handle it. I'm so close, but I feel like I'm only getting farther away. I hear the door open at the top of the stairs, and my dad yells down, "C'mon, boy, you're almost there; get up and get it." I get up and start jump-roping, and it's not for a while that the sweat gets going, but it does.

I can barely feel my extremities now. The sweat has come, albeit slower than ever, but it's here, and I know I will have a while to go before I'm done. I keep my eyes closed and keep skipping, tired as hell, wondering if I might just fall asleep. I do lose awareness of what I'm doing a few times and trip, but I have to hop back up every time. I've never hurt this much in my life. I want to run away. For a split second, I think about getting out of here. I wonder if I could make it on my own.

I stop at noon. I'd taken a few breaks, but now I feel good. I've been sweating for such a long time, and frankly, I don't give a fuck if I am over 135 because this is it. I won't eat or drink anything if I have to. I towel myself off and wait a bit before stepping on the scale, making sure every ounce of fluid leaves my body. When I am completely dry, I take a deep breath and step ever so lightly on the scale.

135.2. I'm good. With six hours to go before weigh-in, all I have to do now is just wait for that last fifth of a pound to go on its own. I can't eat or drink anything; it's too risky. But I've come this far. If I could, I'd spit, but I have nothing left. I need to sleep.

As I walk up the stairs, I tell my dad the news. He shrugs his shoulders at me as if he's disappointed.

"If that's how you wanna do it, then that's how you're gonna do it."

As if on cue, the phone rings. I slump in a chair by the kitchen table to wait for my dad so we can wrap up this miserable conversation, and I feel myself falling asleep until I hear my dad say Coach Thurston's name. I perk up immediately. "No, I think he's okay," my dad says over and over again, and then I know they're talking about weight. This has never happened before. Suddenly, my dad sighs and says, "Yes, just a second," covers the mouthpiece on the phone, gives me that same look he gave me at dinner, and mouths with a little whisper to go along, "Be a man." I nod my head and take the phone.

"How you doing, Tyler?" Coach asks, kinda more concerned sounding than usual.

I tell him I'm fine, trying to sound fine when I do it, but my voice cracks. He says I've been cutting a lot of weight this week, huh? Terry had to walk me down the stairs yesterday? Yeah, you know how it is. Any nosebleeds? Nah.

"Interesting," he says, then a silence. I don't say a word. Don't know what he's driving at, but then he comes out with it.

"Listen, buddy, was thinking of bumping you up to 140 ... I don't think you'll have the wind to go with Stetter with this cut. What do you think?"

My mind goes blank. All week, I've been thinking about two things: Stetter and 135. Some other NA guy and 140 are foreign to me, but I also feel like shit, and I could end my suffering now if I wanted to, and as much as I want to beat Stetter, there's that little part of me that's scared. And this other part of me that is fantasizing about water, and more water, and a cheeseburger.

"Who would go 135?" My dad grimaces when I say this,

and I remember what's gotta be done.

"We throw it to the dogs. You take over for Allen at 140."

"No can do, Coach," I muster, and then I realize I gotta convince him, so I tell him what I've been convincing myself all week, "I have every intention to dethrone the king tonight."

"Attaboy!" Coach Thurston yells. He had just wanted me to convince him, I thought. He didn't wanna move me. I'm still good. I give my dad the phone. He laughs with Coach Thurston, hangs up the phone, and slaps me on the back, but I know he hasn't forgotten that I'm two-tenths over.

I tell him I'm taking a nap. He says he'll wake me up at 3 PM.

Somehow, this time, I am able to fall asleep almost immediately, and I actually dream about the bright lights.

* * *

Of course, like I said, waiting was the most painful part, especially when you had made it down. It's almost like you'd be better off getting down right before the weigh-in. I just never wanted to take that chance. But I think waiting is even more painful than the cutting. I was anxious. So, I don't know if that anxiety carried over into my everyday life. Sometimes, I get jittery when I wait for people or even at work when I am awaiting something important. I've been really anxious lately. My kid's got a big match coming up, and he can barely keep it together now, but I don't know if that's it. It's gotta be something. Or maybe it's nothing at all.

* * *

When my dad wakes me up, I can't move. He is standing there above me, telling me to get up and get ready to go. I tell him I can't and then correct myself when I see his face.

"Help me up. I can barely move."

He reaches down to help me to my feet.

"It's okay. You're almost there. Be tough, Tyler. Be tough."

I get up, and we trudge downstairs together to the scale very slowly. I strip naked in front of my father. It's nothing weird. I'm used to it. I step on the scale, and it flits back and forth between 135 and 135.1.

"Good," he says, "You'll be okay. You've got a few more hours."

I breathe a sigh of relief. He helps me put my stuff together in a bag, and we go out to the pick-up. I can't help but notice how cold it is. It gives you this empty feeling. Like you're doing this brutal thing to yourself, and even when you go to step outside for a moment, you're still taken over by this cold, empty feeling. It puts this fear in you. Like everyone will all be crowded into the warm gym to see you because it's cold outside, so all the attention is on you. I can't quite explain it. It makes me feel weird inside.

When we get to the gym, there are a few cars there, and I can see the North Alleghany bus. The bus gives me chills a bit. It reminds me of what is ahead. Stetter. I wonder if he is nervous as hell, too, or if this is just another walk in the park. I try to swallow, but I obviously still can't. I say goodbye to my dad when we get into the gym, and he goes to sit in the stands and read the program or the newspaper. All he ever says is, "Good luck," and this time isn't any different. I had been expecting something like, hey, this guy is beatable, or just wrestle your match, but there was none of that. I am on my own, like usual.

I'd heard that Stetter was a killer. That's the word you use for someone who doesn't take his time. Stetter goes right for the jugular. He is all about humiliation, the quick pin, the embarrassing, fancy moves when he earns it. He inflicts pain. He goes the extra mile to make the match painful for his opponent, whether it be emotionally or physically, or both; he doesn't really care. I remembered Coach Thurston making me relax before when facing good opponents by saying, "Don't worry, Tyler, he's not a killer. He'll give you a shot." I wonder if Stetter will even "give me a shot."

I walk down into the locker room feeling like I want to shit my pants. It would be a nice thing to happen because then I'd be able to eat, but it's like I feel like shitting my pants, but I know it won't actually happen. Not my favorite feeling. My teammates can see the look on my face, and they know to leave me alone. I don't want to talk to them either. Weigh-in is in a couple hours, so in the meantime, people are going into the wrestling room, which is next to the gym, to cut off last-minute weight. Either that or they are hanging out in the locker room or checking their weight. I decide that if I need to cut weight, I'll wait until 5 PM, and if I still need to lose a tenth, I'll go suck it up and build a sweat. I sit at my locker and wait, feeling worse than I ever have in my life, thinking about Stetter, until 5 PM when Coach Thurston comes in with a bunch of the guys who have been up in the wrestling room. They are drenched in sweat.

"All the guys in the lineup tonight, let's go check weight right now."

No one says a word. We all get up and line up according to our weight class, from 103 to 285. Being 135 puts me toward the front. I pray to God that the scale will just say 135 so I don't have to worry anymore. Losing a tenth of a pound is the worst when you're sucked out. It doesn't just happen magically. You need to work hard to build a sweat, and it's all for a tenth of a pound. After our 130-pounder steps off the scale, Coach Thurston gives me a hard look.

"Lookin' good, Mariotti. Lookin' lean."

It's the only good thing that comes out of this. Sucking all the weight and the water, it makes you real lean. It makes you look good.

I close my eyes and step on the scale. I wait for Coach Thurston to say something. When he doesn't, I peek one eye open, and my heart feels like butterflies.

It says 135. I breathe a sigh of relief. Coach Thurston gives me a nod, and I go back into the locker room to put my head in my hands and think. I just do that for the next hour until the real weigh-in occurs.

* * *

The realization that changed everything ... well, I thought it had already occurred. There had come a time when I thought it would all be worth it if I just made it my life. That it was the most important thing that could ever matter to me and that, eventually, I would find the reason why. For a while, I think I just wanted my father to like me so badly. I think that's why I stuck with it while I was young, at least. I knew I would question it, but I just stuck it in the back of my mind that the time would come when I'd say, okay, this is why it was worth it. This is the moment that will make wrestling useful to my life somehow, outside of the arena. But in the moment, I don't know if I was thinking about that consciously.

I outperformed my dad, that's for sure. But I feel useless now. I'd give a ton of it back just to be 18 again. And I want my kid to realize that, but right now, not later. Then again, that was my experience, so I don't really know if pushing him is right for him. Do you think that's why I am going nuts?

* * *

Here I am, thinking, tapping my toes because any second now, we will weigh in and my suffering will be over. I have three bottles of water in front of me and two bagels. I am ready to devour it all. Right now, I feel like I'd be able to do that and some. But Coach Thurston says we can't get bloated, we'll get cramps, you gotta stay disciplined.

Plus, I know you get big eyes when you're sucked out. I don't know if I'm more anxious to drink some water or see Stetter.

Finally, Coach Thurston tells us to get up, and we all follow him to the end of the locker room where the scales are. There are two scales lined opposite of each other because weigh-ins happen face-to-face. I try to figure out which one is Stetter because they're all taking off their clothes, and eventually, I spot him. One of my teammates nudges me in the arm.

"He's big, dude."

I ignore him and look away. I had seen Stetter for an instant. There was not a shred of fat on the guy, and his muscles were enormous. He didn't look sucked out at all. He just looked like a monster. He had this narrow face with a crew cut, all these sharp features. He just looked mean, and he had this passage tattooed across his stomach. It looked like a Bible passage, and I wondered what kind of Bible passage a mean guy would have across his stomach. The only impression I got from Stetter was that he was unforgiving.

I avoid looking at him for as long as I can, but eventually, they call my name, and I take off my underwear and cup my hands over my genitals and strut over to the scale. I can feel his gaze on me as I step on, and as I do get on the scale, I look up to see him. He is staring me squarely in the eyes. It feels like he is staring right through me and telling me he will murder me. I've never seen so much hatred in my life. I stare right back, not for one second looking at the scale as their coach slides the knobs to the 135 part and watches the lever to see if I've made my weight. It's ironic to me that as I step on the scale, after killing myself in my head all week, that I am actually starting to think about the wrestling side of things a little bit for once.

"Good," he says, and I step down, keeping my eyes on Stetter. For a second, I wonder if he will miss weight, and I kind of pray that he does. But then Coach Thurston says, "Good," and Stetter steps down, turns away, and rushes to grab water. I've almost forgotten myself, and I rush back to get mine.

The first water slides down my throat in under three seconds, and I never feel as refreshed as when it happens. I eat one bagel violently after smothering it with cream cheese and then shift my attention back to another water, which I also chug quickly. Our assistant coach, Coach Hudson, a younger guy, is eyeing me carefully as I do this.

"I know you had a tough time this week, Mariotti, but take it easy. One more water will do it."

I nod my head, and though I have to pause halfway through drinking the third water, I know I could go for more. But it will have to wait. I try to put it out of my mind that I've gained over three pounds in 60 seconds and that soon, the process will start all over again. But it will have to wait as well. I am feeling better. Suddenly, I forget how horrible I've felt all week.

I put on my things excitedly, and when I finish, I wait for the rest of my teammates. Our two captains get up to give us a final talk. This time, I am listening closely. Next year, I know, that will be me up there giving those talks, though I don't know if I could ever be as good as our current captains, Randy and Travis. Randy is our 130, right below me, so I face him a lot. It's weird because he used to win, but this year, I have been dominating. I think it's demoralizing for him to lose as a captain. Travis is our 152, and he is the most popular kid in school. He is a three-time All-Stater in PA, and that's a big deal, even though he's never won it all.

*   *   *

Yeah, I relied on others. We all did. Maybe that's why I am relying on you now. But you just wanted this sense of security, you know? Like we're all in this together. I wanted that from my dad. That's why the victories were sweet; I'd earn his affection back. He stayed like that forever for everything, and it always drove me to work hard and be successful. Kinda sad, huh? I was surprised, but he never held it against me that I quit wrestling in college. I ended up at Pittsburgh, not Johnstown. He was so proud of my other successes. And then he had a grandson to watch. He got to see some of his varsity matches, and the three of us have had some beers together, but my dad died last year right before the State tournament, and I think that's messing with me. I'd be lying if I said that wasn't another reason I'm here, and I think his death is keeping my son invested.

But here's the thing. I never told my dad that my kid hates it. He's an artsy kid. He wants to be in plays and theater and stuff. I don't get it, so I know my dad wouldn't. I wanted to protect him.

I can't believe I'm going to tell you this because I haven't told anyone, not even my father before he died, but I trust you.

I just feel so unsatisfied all of a sudden, like nothing adds up anymore. Like nothing is worthwhile. Kinda like I miss that part where everything else goes away, and it's just you and the you in your head, you know, with everything blocked out. The you versus you that really shows you who you are, how you are, gets things done. It's just a feeling you never have. I mean, I'm sure you have others just like me.

My dad ain't here anymore. So, I sat my son down the other day. I grabbed his shoulders, looked him in the eyes, and told him, "I want you to be your own man."

* * *

Randy gives a short talk, but it's Travis who really lights us up. He is up there telling us how everyone is upstairs and how you can't leave nothing behind because you've put too much on the line. He keeps saying that anything is possible, so go and make it happen. And then he says the same thing he said yesterday, that we will remember this night for the rest of our lives, so we have to make it a good memory. We just have to because you don't wanna live the rest of your life scarred by a bad one. We're all fired up when we get in to give a cheer and go up, and then the feeling overcomes me.

As we're walking in unison up the stairs, there is an electric feeling. It's the combination of being all torn up inside with nerves and being anxious about whatever is about to happen. It's like you are in control of this amazing thing. And everything all seems to make sense. The noise our shoes make against the metal staircase somehow puts this energy in me. The way we are marching like soldiers going into battle, silent and scared, it makes me feel like I'm entitled to something. Now, all of a sudden, I am sweating without even trying. And as we run into the gym as a team for warm-up, I can feel the excitement chill my bones as hundreds of people scream. There is not a single empty place in the gym; it is even difficult to weave through the crowd for us to do our warm-up. Soon, the lights dim, and a special light turns on and hovers on top of the mat so that it is the only thing being lit up. Suddenly, the surreal feeling of the whole thing goes away because I am in the dark and I can't see the crowd. I'm no longer dizzy with thought and feeling because everyone goes quiet as they do the national anthem. As soon as it ends, we shake hands with our opponents. I don't look at Stetter. He was an asshole during the weigh-in, and now, with everyone cheering and Carly sitting in the front row with her pom-poms, I just want to kick his ass. Fuck his accomplishments, I say to myself. Tonight is its own night. The past does not matter. It's something Randy had said in the locker room because NA is favored to beat us.

My match is third, so I immediately go into the wrestling room as the match begins. Randy comes with me because he is on deck. We don't speak to each other. In the darkness, we shadow wrestle, as if we are wrestling an actual opponent, but really just going through the motions. We jump rope, we skip, we do anything to build the sweat. It's so when the match comes, that you get that first big sweat out of you, so you won't be shocked when you get tired in the match. I hear a lot of cheering and a loud thud, and I know we've won the first match. As they call Randy's name, I don't say a word; I just feel the butterflies creeping in my stomach.

This is the time when the fear kicks in. The fear of losing it. Not of losing, exactly, but losing it altogether. It's the time when you feel like you might just be too tired to go on, and then lose and feel like it was all in your control to push through, and then you live with that for the rest of your life. And everyone sees it, and they think you're soft. It's the most frightening thing. It's the fear of second-guessing yourself or that the six minutes will somehow be too long. I keep telling myself that when the match starts, six minutes later, it will be over. And that's that. I'll just have to give it my all. I mean, I'll remember it forever.

I'm sweating bullets, and Randy's match is still going on, but I know it must be over soon because I can barely stand straight. I can't help but start to take off my outer warm-ups now. Finally, I hear a lot of applause, and though I don't know if Randy has won or lost, I know the match is over. I hear the PA announcer begin to speak. As soon as he says Stetter's name, I take off my shirt and shorts so it is just me in my singlet with my headgear and my mouthpiece. This is it. When he says my name, I come through the door.

When they see me, they go crazy. I can barely see them because they are dimly lit by the light shining over the mat. I can see my father in the middle of it all, just looking plain but cheering for me. I am just running now, and I'm not thinking about anything else except that I have just torn off my clothes and everyone can see me in this almost naked state, but I am not ashamed. I feel pride in feeling like the warrior, that they are all looking at my body in awe, which is shiny because of the way my skin glistens when I sweat. I feel like a superhero, and I revel in the fact that people are watching me, my every move, envious of my body because I am so sucked out and strong-looking.

I could think about how winning would be the ultimate victory or how losing would be the ultimate defeat, but I am locked in. I am the warrior. Even though I have done nothing but think leading up to this match, this is the moment of no thought as I slap Coach Thurston's hand and run out to the center of the mat and hear the noise. Then comes the time when everything stops, and I can no longer hear anyone but myself in this very moment, standing here, ready to go for six minutes on pure instinct. I stop to notice Stetter and feel a bit intimidated, but only for a moment because the ref is about to blow the whistle and I am tantalized by the bright lights.

*   *   *

Yes, I do think that night was the time everything changed, where everything else just faded away, and somehow—I'll never forget it—it was all just worth it.

WHY I DON'T BELIEVE —

The day I lost my innocence came shortly after I became a man. My Bar Mitzvah was still fresh in my mind, and I had deemed myself to be filled with righteousness. I was naïve then. I hadn't even kissed a girl yet.

My fastidious nature had distinguished me from my classmates. I had been shielded all along by my parents, who prohibited hard candy when I was five, PG-13 movies when I was ten, and television before homework when I was thirteen. It was because of this—my sheltered life and my focus on academics—that my parents encouraged me to apply for private schooling.

To me, the whole ordeal was a distraction from my everyday life. I was short-sighted. The application process was not exciting but mandatory, nor did I realize the long-term implications of the decisions that lay ahead. I knew I might follow my brother at one of the most prestigious and rigid boys' schools in Massachusetts. I also knew I might receive a co-educational boarding experience at a more elitist school in New Hampshire, a country club atmosphere further from home. Or I would remain in public school. It didn't matter too much to me then. I just liked playing sports and hanging out with my friends.

But for my parents, who had already lost their innocence, my parents who knew to look ahead for me, my future was everything. And that was why I had to spend a weekend in the Berkshires, a mountainous and rural area of Western Massachusetts. It would be beautiful this time of year, they told me, with the snow and the deer. Maybe I would see deer like the ones by our home.

It was all so Mrs. Garrison—my best friend's mother and a prominent figure in the Phillips Exeter community—could get to know me better. Mrs. Garrison had offered to write a recommendation on my behalf for Exeter; indeed, it was a strong relationship between our mothers that had sparked a whole friendship between our families. Her encounters with me were only inconsequential, and she needed to spend more time with me so she could give a better account of my character. It was really just a formality, she said, but her family was going on vacation anyway. So, we would spend a weekend at their vacation home in the Berkshires. But then, Mrs. Garrison was unable to attend at the last second due to a charity golf tournament she had signed up for and completely forgotten about. I imagined her pleading with Mr. Garrison to let me go with them anyway, begging him to write the letter for her, because a few days later, we got a phone call with the change of plans: Mr. Garrison would be writing the letter for me, and he was looking forward to getting to know me better.

The Garrisons were family friends of ours. They, like us, lived in the same town of superlatives. It was one of the wealthiest, the smallest, the most suburban, and whitest towns in Massachusetts. Our parents had met at some school or town function. They had a boy my age, Jack, whom I went to school with, and an older boy my brother's age, Arthur, who was a standout scholar-athlete at Phillips-Exeter. Where our families had no overlap was with their third child, their eleven-year-old daughter, Rachel. They all had blond hair and blue eyes except Rachel, so she was unique even within her own family. But she was striking nonetheless; you could tell she would grow up to be a pretty girl.

For me, this trip was more about playing with Jack than getting to know anybody. When my parents kissed me goodbye and packed my sleeping bag snugly in the trunk of Mr. Garrison's car, my focus turned immediately to Jack, who sat between Rachel and me in the backseat. Up in the front, Mr. Garrison would talk to Arthur about his current hockey season and upcoming lacrosse season for the whole three-hour trip, occasionally pausing to ask questions to Jack or me. Sometimes, these questions bordered on the absurd, as I noticed that Mr. Garrison seemed uncomfortable with me, checking on me from time to time through his rearview mirror. Rachel was sullenly listening to music and watching the snow-dusted trees pass by her window. Mrs. Garrison was, of course, playing golf, but she had hugged us all before we left, starting with Rachel and working her way up to Mr. Garrison, who smiled meekly after kissing her on the cheek.

They were all unlike my family. They were the typical All-American family. They exuded Aryan features and athleticism and loved Nantucket and majestic Labrador retrievers. They were looser than my family, more talkative, less concerned. My family was more reserved. We were one of the only Jewish families in town. I often felt different from everyone else. But Jack and I got along because we had a lot in common. It was sports that we liked. We played on town soccer teams together. We were the fastest kids in our grade. We traded baseball cards. He was partial to being active outdoors—like mountain biking, for example. He was a little rougher around the edges than me; scrapes and bruises were no big deal for him. I was a little softer, but we were too young to weigh these differences too heavily. I think, deep down, I wanted to be more like him.

Toward the end of the car ride, we brushed through a labyrinth of pine trees up a narrow, ice-ridden pathway for what seemed like a long time. The car turned silent. Rachel had fallen asleep, but the rest of us had ceased our conversations as if to watch Mr. Garrison in wonder as he navigated through the cold. Either that, or we were trying not to curse him as he tread ever so delicately on the glimmering surface beneath us. Snow was piled waist-high on either side of the car because of the plows, leaving a slick trail of ice underneath.

"Don't worry, boys. I've done this hundreds of times," Mr.

Garrison said, his eyes fixed firmly on Jack and me in his rear-view mirror. I couldn't help but notice how handsome he was. The thought didn't enter my mind like that. No, the word "handsome" wouldn't have come into my head because I was only on the cusp of maturity and sexuality. But he reminded me of a superhero. He seemed young, full of vitality. His hair was brushed back, and he was wearing a salmon-colored, tight-fitting, collared polo from a designer. He looked like someone I would see on television.

The bumpy trek led us to the house, just as Mr. Garrison promised. "There she is," he said calmly. I looked at the house in amazement and gasped audibly.

Mr. Garrison chuckled. Jack forcefully nudged Rachel awake with his elbow, and she returned the favor with a sharp glare. They got out on the other side as I stared at the house. It was bigger than their primary house, but it was more isolated, and somehow, I found it more interesting. You could tell it was an old house that had been renovated. Though it had flair as a traditional home in the midst of nature, parts of the home seemed new, like the abutting section that looked out over the lake. We had been studying Henry David Thoreau in school at the time, and a weird, random thought crossed my mind that maybe Walden Pond was cooler than I thought. Maybe this would be even more fun than I expected.

We gathered our belongings out from the trunk and went inside. It was just as palatial inside as it appeared from the outside. The shiny wooden floors reflected sunlight from the rectangular-paned windows that overlooked the lake. The white walls were adorned with family photographs. A large framed photograph of Mr. and Mrs. Garrison with one of their dogs hung right in front of me by the staircase. They were enthusiastic, wearing gray turtlenecks, holding their dog in a funny position in what looked like the middle of an open field. I noticed their forced expressions. Their white teeth.

Jack led me to the opposite side of the house. We entered

a wooden corridor that seemed much older than the rest of the house. There were actual logs—splintered logs—holding up this section of the home. It had a musty scent, but I welcomed the change, breathing in deeply and exhaling with a short sigh. We walked up a thin timber staircase into a loft with two beds that overlooked the living room below. Jack smiled at me from over his shoulder, set down his things by his bed, and jabbed me in the arm.

"Let's play some hockey," he said, the gap between his front teeth more apparent than usual. Before I could say anything, I was following Jack back down the wooden staircase toward the entrance of the house. He took an unexpected turn by the coat room down a hallway I had not initially noticed. The hall veered at the very end to the left, but only briefly, for there was a door there that led to the basement.

We hustled down the pine-colored steps, which creaked uneasily beneath us. Jack flipped a light switch at the bottom of the stairs that dimly lit the whole basement except the far end, which contained storage and, in the corner, a fully made pink bed with a light bulb overhead. There was a little string connecting to the bulb to turn it on and off. The basement was grungy and unfinished, but there was a large, open space for us to play hockey. The far wall bore scattered white scratch marks from the pucks or balls that Jack had shot against it with his stick. He had drawn a hockey net onto the wall with chalk.

He propped a stick against my stomach while I gazed around the room. Jack threw his goalie mask on and started to put on his pads. I noticed the multitude of wooden doors and wondered where they led. They were surely part of the original house by the looks of their exteriors, and there was something very mysterious about that. I wanted to explore—maybe there was a hidden treasure. I would suggest it later, I thought to myself; in the meantime, I had other inquiries.

"Why is there a pink bed?" I asked, smirking.

Jack looked down at the floor.

"Rachel used to sleep there sometimes," he said sheepishly. Realizing the awkward silence, he added, looking back up at me, "Because of the renovation. It makes our hockey arena less cool."

"Oh," I replied slowly, "That's too bad."

"Did you see the Bruins game last night?" Jack asked suddenly, his goalie mask hanging over his head so he could see me better.

"Canadiens, right?"

"Yeah. Did you see the fight?"

I had seen the fight. I loved the fights.

"Yeah …"

I was cut off by Arthur, who came barreling down the stairs. Without hesitation, he started hitting Jack, who tried, to no avail, to throw some defensive jabs back.

"Yeah, I saw the fight too! It was all like this, you little faggot!" Arthur yelled while Jack giggled. Soon, Jack's giggling turned into soft wincing, and Arthur paused as Rachel shouted for us to keep it down from the top of the stairs. Arthur smiled at us and left, threatening to pick up Rachel, who shrieked and scampered at the sound of Arthur's voice.

Jack and I played alone for the next couple of hours, talking about nothing but hockey, wondering if the Boston Bruins would ever win the Stanley Cup again.

* * *

That evening, we were called to dinner by Mr. Garrison. He had ordered in pizza.

"There are pizza places out here?" I asked furtively.

Mr. Garrison gave his patent movie-star chuckle.

"There are pizza places everywhere, Nate."

"There's no pizza places on the moon," Jack retorted. Mr. Garrison looked at Jack with a feigned expression of disappointment and then laughed. He put his hand on Jack's thigh, making him squirm a bit furtively.

"I should be more careful about what I say next time."

So, we ate pizza and talked and watched the snow spread gently over the lake.

After dinner, Arthur, Jack, and Rachel went to play board games. I tried to join them, but Mr. Garrison, who had just left the dirty dishes in the sink, tapped me lightly on the shoulder.

"Sorry, Nate, but I heard from your mother that you are learning chess. Would you like to play a game with me before you play with them?"

I looked at Jack from across the room for help, but he was setting up a game with Arthur and Rachel. I saw the chess table beside us. It looked expensive. The marble gleamed at me, beckoning me to play. I didn't want to, but I knew I had to. I looked from the table back up at Mr. Garrison.

"Sure, I'll give it a shot," I said with a reluctant smile.

He turned to set up the pieces, and I tried to look and see if Jack was having fun across the room. I sat myself cautiously on one side of the square table upon a slab of rock. I wondered if the seats for the table were actually just found in the nearby wilderness or if they had some company carve the rocks. I decided it was more likely the latter.

Mr. Garrison got out a couple of pieces of paper and some pencils, offering one of each to me so that I could keep track of the moves. I pretended that this methodical practice was familiar, though I had not reached the level where I wrote down moves yet. He also removed a clock from a hidden drawer in the table. I had not played with a clock before, but again, I faked preparedness when Mr. Garrison urged me to make the first move. I wanted him to think well of me.

It did not take long for me to discover that Mr. Garrison was an experienced player. He made deft decisions, pausing to think only shortly, as if he had memorized every possible scenario, occasionally mumbling a word or two to me or, more often, to himself. He would routinely consider the board, move a piece, punch the clock, and record it all on his sheet of paper.

Then he would fold his arms and stare at me, always sporting a friendly gaze. Occasionally, he would study the piece of paper as well. I, on the other hand, was constantly thinking. My piece of paper did not mesmerize me, but Mr. Garrison did. It was like he knew something I didn't. What was I supposed to understand with each of his moves? I guessed each time. The results were negative, but only for a while.

I had nearly given up when I noticed that the board had opened up some opportunities for me to take some of his pieces. I had only been taking lessons for a few months with some middle-aged Russian man at the behest of my mother, but I was smart enough to know basic situations, and this looked like one of them. I took his rook.

"Good move," he said. He had begun talking to me more and asking questions about what I liked to do rather than being preoccupied with the game. It was as if he had already convinced himself that he had won earlier on in the match. "Thanks," I said and blushed. Our exchange went on much like that. He asked me if I had a girlfriend, prompting Jack to shout from the other side of the room that I didn't like girls.

"Not yet," I said as I grinned, "but I'm working on it."

"Ah, I see ..." he said slowly, casually moving a piece and hitting the clock. With my next move, I earned checkmate. He had let me win the game.

"Very impressive, Nate. You are a smart boy," he said, standing up from the table and extending his hand. I shook it, felt the firmness of his shake, and, for the first time, noticed how tall he was. I barely reached his chest.

We walked over to the others who were finishing up their game. Mr. Garrison placed his hands on Rachel's shoulders and bent over to give her a kiss on the cheek. "I'm off to bed, everyone. Nate, the dogs have the lay of the land on the main floor, and Arthur is sleeping in the loft on the other side of the house. You and Jack have the loft on this end. You'll have everything you need right up there: video games, TV, a fridge. You won't really want to leave there, to be honest."

He was beaming. I nodded my head.

"I'll see you in the morning."

He gave Arthur a light pat on the back and came around the other side of the sofa to give Jack a kiss goodnight. Jack squirmed away when Mr. Garrison bent over, embarrassed because I was watching. I think he was also a little jealous that his father seemed to think so highly of me.

When they finished their game (which Arthur won), Jack and I went to the loft to go to sleep. I changed into pajamas, and when I came back, Jack had a mischievous grin on his face as he sat facing me on the far bed. He was holding a magazine in his hand.

"What?" I asked, laughing a little myself.

"It's a *Hustler*," he was grinning again, his freckles beaming.

"You just found it?"

"No, dude, of course not. I keep it under my bed here. Arthur gave it to me last year."

It looked like that was the truth. The tattered pages barely clung to the spine of the magazine; indeed, pages were ripped from wear or sticky from God-knows-what.

"Oh," I responded stoically, "cool."

He gaped at me as I started tugging on the blanket of my bed.

"Well, let's look at it," he said. I sighed and paced over to his bed hesitantly, seating myself on his left side. He scrolled through the magazine. I had never seen anything like it before. Pornography scared me. The graphic imagery of men and women made me curious. I felt confused sometimes, disgusted other times, mildly aroused rarely, and sometimes all of these emotions at once.

"This one is my favorite," he said, turning to a page focused on a vagina. The woman's fingers were stretching it wide, and she looked like she was moaning. I felt like throwing up. And then I felt confused. I thought I was supposed to like vaginas.

"Yeah, that's awesome; what else is there?" I said all at once, not pausing whatsoever, hoping for him to turn the page to something else—or even better, shut the magazine. He did just that.

"I dunno," he said, bringing the battered folds together. "There's a bunch of stuff. We can look at it tomorrow."

I had trouble sleeping that night. I thought about the naked women and tried to have an erection. I wondered if I was gay.

That painful experience was abruptly but temporarily removed from my memory when Arthur jolted us awake in the morning.

"C'mon, guys, let's try out the slide! Get up, let's go!"

He was wearing a bathing suit and had a towel over his shoulder. He was mostly poking Jack to try to get him up, but he would occasionally come over to do the same to me.

"It's so cold, though," Jack said groggily.

"That's what makes it fun. We can go in the hot tub afterward," Arthur shot back.

Jack's face lit up, and he curved his hips so that he was sitting upward to face Arthur.

"Where's Rachel?"

"Screw Rachel. She's probably with Dad, picking up groceries for dinner or the game later or something like that," Arthur replied.

Jack got out of bed and rummaged through his backpack for a bathing suit. "I didn't bring a bathing suit," I muttered.

"It's okay, I brought a couple," Jack said, offering one to me with one hand. "Thanks," I groaned. I was still tired but mildly excited and anxious about testing out the "slide."

After we got changed, we tiptoed out the backdoor because it was so cold outside. Then I saw it: a slide had been built over the boathouse over the lake. There must have been a thirty-foot drop. This was the kind of activity Jack and Arthur loved to do. I, on the other hand, had a fear of heights. I shivered on the dock while Jack and Arthur rushed to the ladder that led up over the boathouse. I noticed how toned they each were and how Jack was just a blossoming version of Arthur, who, it now occurred to me, strongly resembled his father. Arthur's long, blond hair violently tossed as he pushed Jack aside when they got to the ladder. When he got up to the top, he yelled excitedly at us.

"The slide is iced over! Oh my God. It's going to be so fast."

I was too distracted by the frigidity of the air to be overly concerned with the slide. It intimidated me. I didn't want to ride on it and immediately started thinking of ways I could get myself out of doing so without taking too much abuse. I focused on the hot tub in front of me on the deck, which Arthur had started to heat up before we got outside. I wanted to just sit down in it for a while and think. Looking at these strong boys, so spirited and so free, I suddenly—desperately—wanted to get away.

My attention turned back to Arthur when I heard his rump collapse against the slide. He was riding down at an uncomfortably fast pace and yelping the whole way. This all ended with a resounding splash. Jack and I waited with trepidation for Arthur to reach the lake's surface. After about ten seconds, Jack yelled over to me from the top of the boathouse.

"Where is he?"

He was running around frantically on the top of the boathouse. I, too, started jogging over to the lakeside.

"Where is he?!" Jack started yelling over and over again. My heart was pounding, and I was quickly awakened from my anxious stupor; the cold air started to prickle my skin, and soon I was feeling surprisingly warm.

I started to panic. Jack was screaming and asserting that he would go into the water to look for Arthur. I looked between him and the house and wondered if I should dial 911. But just as Jack sat down on the slide so he could go get Arthur, a blob of yellow hair reached the lake's surface.

"Haha! I got you guys!" Arthur grinned widely.

"That wasn't funny, Arthur!" Jack screamed as he glided down the slide and into the water. He seemed to have quickly forgotten his fears.

"C'mon, Nate ... hop in!" Arthur yelled. When Jack reached the surface, he made wild gesticulations while raving about how fun it was. Like Arthur, he turned to me to encourage me to use the slide. We bickered about my participation for quite some time. I tried explaining to them my fear of heights, but they said that I was afraid of spiders, too, and how could I be afraid of everything? I had been worried about this moment from the get-go. I knew that going on a trip into nature with these people, inevitably, a moment like this would arise where my own personal fears and anxieties would be aired out loud in an uncomfortably public way.

Eventually, I resolved the matter by entering the hot tub. They quietly succumbed, and each took a few more turns on the slide before joining me, dripping wet from the lake and hugging themselves tightly with their arms. I took in the scenery around us: snow-covered pine trees encircled the lake with enormous moss-covered rocks at their side. There were other massive homes of varying shapes on the opposite side of the lake.

"You missed out on a good slide," Arthur said.

"Yeah," Jack added, "that was a lot of fun."

I splayed my arms out on the sides of the hot tub, letting my body absorb the heat as I enjoyed the stark contrast between the cold weather and the warmth of my body. I tilted my head skyward, and before closing my eyes, I noticed something. It was Rachel, looking at me from behind the blinds in the house. When she saw me notice her, she immediately shut the blinds and moved away.

We sat in silence for several minutes, and then Arthur spoke to us with his familiar condescending tone.

"So, have you fags nailed any girls yet? Or do you still beat it to the *Hustler* I gave you for your twelfth birthday?"

"Of course we have," Jack argued defiantly. "I kissed Alyssa Torre at Evan's party last weekend in spin-the-bottle."

I started to feel uneasy again, just like when Jack pulled out the magazine the previous evening. It was not that I didn't like girls. In fact, I had just started liking them. But I was shy around them, and I felt awkward about my lack of experience in dealing with them. I tended to be their friend, not the boy they wanted to kiss. Jack seemed further along than me with that stuff, but Arthur wasted no time in bringing Jack down.

"Ha, Alyssa Torre. You know, I banged her older sister all the time for like a whole month. What a slut. Guess it runs in the family if her little sister is kissing guys like you."

Jack laughed and splashed water on Arthur. I wondered how women came so easily to Arthur. I didn't think he was trying to impress us—why would he have to? He was a handsome, athletic boy, much like his father, and I began to see how he could win girls over so easily. But why did he move from one girl to another all the time? When I asked during our conversation if he had a girlfriend, he merely replied, "Never."

It was not much longer before Mr. Garrison came home. He opened the sliding door and, with one arm, held up a brown paper bag of groceries, his other arm draped around Rachel's neck. She played with her necklace and looked at the rusting metal of the hot tub's exterior while he spoke to us.

"There you guys are. Arthur, I trust you boys didn't go on the slide while I was out."

"Course not, Dad. Jack's a pussy anyway; he wouldn't go on even if he had the chance."

Jack looked at me and wanted to say something, but he was smart enough to know that he would incriminate himself by saying anything. He bit his lip and gave Arthur a dirty look. I laughed. So did Mr. Garrison, but then he coughed and turned serious.

"Well, uh, you know that's not nice talk, Arthur. And Jack is a big boy now." Jack blushed the same crimson color that I saw the night before when Mr. Garrison tried to kiss him on the cheek. There was a pause. We all looked at each other. "Well, c'mon, guys," Mr. Garrison said, flipping his wrist upward so he could look at his watch. "It's game time soon. I got us some food. Let's go in and watch the game and eat."

We dried off and watched football all afternoon. Mr. Garrison asked us if we wanted to go hunting or snow-shoeing. Arthur said, "No," so we just stayed by the television. Mr. Garrison reclined in a chair and gripped a beer. Rachel had disappeared. She was keeping to herself somewhere.

Dinner that night was strange. Mr. Garrison had cooked a roast, but the meal was sub-par, and everyone chewed slowly and forcefully amidst the silence. Mr. Garrison tried to overcome the somber mood by asking me questions, but my mind was elsewhere. I wondered where all the rooms led to in the basement. Maybe the Garrisons didn't appreciate the mystery and opportunity that was before them in their very own home. Maybe they were too busy trailblazing the outdoors, building death-machine slides by the lake, and biking through the woods, throwing rocks at bears. Maybe they hadn't explored their own home yet. Maybe they were afraid or unconcerned. Probably unconcerned.

"No, Mr. Garrison, we just have a couple of cats. I mean, three cats."

"Ah, I see. Well, that's nice. Though dogs are beautiful animals; they really are ..." his voice trailed off at the sight of Rachel, who sighed heavily and put her fork down.

"Yes, darling?" Mr. Garrison tilted his head. Rachel was shaking.

"I'm ... I'm just not hungry," she muttered, looking everywhere but at her father.

"Well, would you like dessert?" he asked her, unfazed by his obvious lack of culinary skills. She smiled immediately and said, "Yes."

Mr. Garrison went to the kitchen counter and whipped up the best-looking ice cream sundae I had ever seen. I wanted one, but I did not ask.

"Here you go, sweetheart."

Rachel smiled.

"Any boys in your life?" Arthur asked, grinning.

"Just you two," Rachel said in between frantic bites.

"What about me?" Mr. Garrison asked, pretending to be offended.

"I meant you three. And Nate, of course," she corrected herself, looking at me. I blushed. Mr. Garrison kissed her on the cheek. She did not squirm away like Jack.

It was then that I decided Mr. Garrison was truly infallible.

I was not tired when Jack and I ascended the stairs to our beds that evening. We would be going home the next afternoon, and I felt like it all flew by too fast. We didn't end up skiing or hunting or doing much related to nature like I had previously expected. We had done some night fishing briefly after dinner, but that was all. Perhaps they thought I would be uncomfortable doing things I wasn't used to doing. I'm not really sure. Maybe they were so used to being outdoors that they wanted to get away from it this time. But that seemed all too ironic.

Jack and I talked to each other in the darkness about everything that crossed our minds. I was grateful that we didn't look at the *Hustler*. We talked a lot about girls, though. I told him who I thought the prettiest three girls were in our grade, and we agreed on the first two, though I suppose I had an odd taste for choosing Becky Winter as my number three because Jack seemed repulsed by that selection. He told me about how one time he walked in on his brother receiving a blowjob from a girl, and since only Arthur noticed him and gave a thumbs-up, he stayed and watched them have sex through the crack in the door. He said he knew everything about sex. He started describing it to me, but he eventually ran out of steam and decided to go to sleep.

I stared uncomfortably at the stuffed moose head that hung directly above me. I wondered if it was real and, if it was, if maybe it could look down on me. Probably not, I decided. And then I wondered what happens to us when we die. Is there even a heaven? Are we judged? And then I wondered about the basement again.

By now, I had to pee, and it had already been an hour since Jack had fallen asleep.

Mr. Garrison was right that we could entertain ourselves in the loft, and we had, but he was wrong when he asserted that we would never have to leave, and that is because the bathroom was downstairs. So, I decided when I went downstairs to use the bathroom that maybe—if I could overcome my fear of the dark—I would explore the basement.

I removed myself silently from my bed, making sure that Jack was still asleep, and crept down the stairs. I was cold, and while hugging myself tightly, I realized a feeling of frightful solitude creeping up within me. The house was dark and empty, and I immediately second-guessed my decision to tour it before departing the next day. After using the bathroom, I walked down the corridor that Jack had led me down before. I took a deep breath when I reached the door and closed my eyes.

I twisted the knob slowly and abruptly let go. I turned around to go back to bed. But then I thought about Arthur and Jack making fun of my fear of heights and spiders, my ineptitude with girls, and my distaste for vaginas. I became angry. I took the doorknob firmly and thrust myself into the darkness.

When I eased the door shut behind me, I realized that the lock on the inner side was broken but covered in tape, and I had masterfully closed it without making a noise. I paused to look for the light switch. I fumbled around for an indeterminable amount of time, praying that I would find something. I did not want to go into the darkness. But I had come this far, and then I realized that there was another light switch at the bottom of the staircase, the one Jack had turned on when we played hockey the day before. If I could just make it to the bottom, I would be alright. I descended further into the darkness.

I gripped the railing on my right and took a step, afraid I might miss one and fall. When my first foot landed, I breathed a sigh of relief. I came down harder with my trail foot, and the wooden board creaked below me ever so silently, sending waves of discomfort throughout my stomach. I studied the still solemnity of the blankness around me, but nevertheless, I continued with more conviction, keeping my eyes closed in fear that something might happen to me on my way down the stairs, that something might jump out at me or that I would be hit suddenly or thrown into panic by some sudden noise. With each step, I felt like my heart skipped a beat. I could feel my hair raised on end in the intense coldness. And then, when I was about halfway down the stairs, I froze entirely at the sound of muffled noises coming from the corner of the basement.

They were soft, shrill cries, and they came infrequently. When I first heard a noise, I stopped in my tracks and felt an icy chill run through me. Something else was down here, and I could not see it in the darkness. I waited, one hand gripping the railing, the other pressed against the wall, and my feet on separate stairs, taking deep breaths with my eyes closed and my mouth shut as my heart fluttered in my chest. I put my other foot down on the stair I had just stepped on and waited, listening, for several minutes. I sat in silence for seemingly endless periods of time before hearing the noise. I thought about leaving but wondered if the creaking noises I had made would only get louder and how exposing my back to the basement would make me feel more vulnerable. I tried to convince myself that the noises were from a heater or some other device. It seemed plausible, and I began to calm down. I opened my eyes and started to brace myself to move forward. Then, when I heard a soft grunt, it became readily apparent to me that these were human noises. Other people were down here.

My mind raced. I did not want to find out what was down there anymore. I lost my ability to think rationally; instead, it felt like a wave was crashing into my mind, dizzying my sight into blurry blackness. I started sweating as I stood there, my cold, wet hands now both clenching the railing. As each noise came, I would tremble a little more. Finally, I determined I had to leave.

The grunting became louder, and I lost my composure. I

needed to leave now before the person or people down there got a hold of me. But in my bold rush to leave, my foot caught the bottom of the stair behind me, forcing me to come down hard on the stair I had been standing on. It made a loud, creaking noise, and all of a sudden, the room—and my mind, which had been crowded by seemingly loud, rushed thoughts— were filled with silence.

"Who is that?" a voice called out from the abyss. The sound made me open my mouth in horror. It was, unmistakably, the voice of Mr. Garrison. For a second, I thought that I could just explain myself, apologize, and forget everything. It was not a stranger, and I had no business knowing what he was doing down here anyway. But what would he think of me? What if he got mad and ... did something? I remained silent, closing my eyes and hoping everything would go away. I hoped he would fall asleep.

I stood there like that for what seemed like hours, listening to my heart dance rapidly in my stomach, then slow down to a calmer, rhythmic beat. I wanted to take a deep breath, but I had to stay as quiet as possible, so I kept sucking in small breaths, exhaling slowly but softly. I opened my eyes, hoping that they would adjust to the darkness, but all I could make out was the rough outlines of shapes in the basement. If Mr. Garrison had decided to come upstairs, he probably could have been within a few feet of me before I would have been able to see any sort of figure. This thought crossed my mind, that I was defenseless and exposed. I felt naked. I felt *violated*.

The light bulb from the corner of the room turned on, and we saw each other shrouded by misty, graying darkness, two somewhat familiar shapes. The light half-illuminated but granulated Mr. Garrison sitting upright and shirtless in a bed next to a blob under the covers beside him. I should have understood, but I was confused about everything back then. He kept his left hand firmly there and looked deeply at me, a scowl on his face. I had never seen him look at me like this. I was only dimly lit, but enough so that Mr. Garrison knew it was me. I started shaking uncontrollably—I would have to confront him now.

"Nate? Is that you?" he said, twisting his head so he could get a better view. He was so obscure in the murky distance that he seemed like a creature, not a man.

I searched for things to say. I considered a last-ditch attempt at escaping since he was not completely sure it was me. In the end, I replied timidly. "Yes. Yes, it's me, Nate."

Mr. Garrison violently reached for the bulb above him and turned it off. My eyes did not adjust appropriately, and I felt myself beginning to tremble as my fear of the dark reasserted itself. I then heard the sound of covers as, presumably, he rushed out of the bed. I wanted to run now, but my feet were glued to the floor.

"What are you doing down here, Nate?" he said in a worried voice, which was clearly approaching me quickly.

"I-I dunno. I got lost looking for the bathroom."

"You know where the bathroom is, Nate," he answered accusingly. Then I heard the creek of the bottom stair. He was coming up the stairs!

"Yeah, I just wanted to ... explore a little bit," I said, trying to cover up for myself, hoping he would not hurt me or yell at me. I heard a creaking sound from right below me. He was only a few steps away now. I tried telling myself that this was not happening, that I had not intruded on him, that I had not seen anything.

"You know curiosity is not always good. It can be bad. Didn't you learn about Adam and Eve? Or do Jews not believe in that?"

He was standing right in front of me now. I could see the outline of his rough exterior, his disappointed face looking down at me.

"Yes. Yes, I did. We do. I'm sorry, Mr. Garrison."

He took a deep breath and placed his hand on my shoulder. The contact made me jump.

"I didn't mean that, Nate. Let's just pretend I never said that, okay? I was a bit startled. Why don't you go on back to bed now, and I'll talk to you about this in the morning," he said, his hand gripping my shoulder blade so hard that I wanted to cry.

"Yes, sir! Yes, Mr. Garrison. Goodnight."

With that, I scampered up the stairs, and for the second straight night, I did not sleep well.

For the second straight morning, I was also rudely awakened. This time, it was Mr. Garrison shaking me to consciousness and whispering my name, and when I saw him, my natural response was to open my mouth to scream until I realized he was not trying to hurt me.

"Nate ... Nate ... wake up. I forgot eggs yesterday. Why don't you come with me so I can get to know you a little better before we go home later today?"

The last thing I wanted to do was talk to Mr. Garrison after the previous evening's fiasco, but I felt like I owed him something. The night before, I had begun to piece together possible reasons for Mr. Garrison's odd behavior, but none of them appealed to me until later that morning when we all sat down for breakfast. I assented anyway—because I had to—and got out of bed to get dressed.

I could not help but shiver as I crawled into the front seat of Mr. Garrison's car, half-asleep. Part of me was worried he was going to drive me somewhere and leave me there, but I didn't know why. He seemed different all of a sudden. Unshaven, more rugged, independent. He was less a superhero now, more a villain. He was more mysterious than the basement, but he also seemed more human than ever before.

We sat in silence for the whole ride to the grocery store. He stole glances at me as if he was hoping to say something, and I was too afraid to initiate any sort of discourse with him as well. Somehow, I was relatively calm about this endeavor, and I attributed that to my extreme fatigue. I looked out my window sorrowfully, hoping to spot a deer or something moving, but all I got was snow and trees.

Our car was the only one in the parking lot when we pulled into the grocery store. Then, Mr. Garrison uttered the first words of our voyage.

"Stay here, Nate. I'll be right back."

He got out of the car. I noted his flannel shirt. It was less stylish than the other clothing he had worn thus far.

While he was gone, I thought about the night before. I had thought about it before drifting off to sleep, but I could not solve the puzzle. What were the noises? Was he masturbating? It seemed plausible. But it sounded like there was another person with Mr. Garrison. Was he ... cheating? No—I would've seen someone. Or maybe they knew the secret entrances and exits of the mysterious basement. Maybe that someone knew the basement very well. And what was all that nonsense about Adam and Eve? I didn't have time to dwell on it all for very long because Mr. Garrison had rushed back to the car with a pack of twelve eggs. The ride back was filled with conversation. He didn't even hesitate when he started up the car.

"So, Nate, why were you going into our basement last night all by yourself?" Well, that's quite simple, I thought to myself. Maybe this wouldn't be so bad.

"I was curious about all the doors, where they go. I forgot to ask Jack about them, and I was running out of time to find out."

"So, it's nothing to do with Jack saying anything to you then?"

Why would Jack say anything to me? I wondered then, and even today, I am not sure I have every detail figured out.

"Nope. But I wish I asked him about it during the day."

"And what did you see or hear when you came downstairs last night?"

I coughed and thought to myself. I would just tell him the truth. I didn't know what else to do.

"I didn't really see anything. Just you when you turned on the light. And some soft noises, perhaps you were snoring; sorry if I woke you up—" I was running on and on before he interrupted.

"Noises?" He raised his eyebrows, looking straight ahead at the road and at me, back and forth.

"Yes, you know, like I said ... probably just snoring or something."

He turned his head and looked at me closely.

"I see." And then silence. I thought I was off the hook, but I could tell he was struggling to say something to me; either that or he knew what he wanted to say but not how to say it. He started biting his nails with his free hand as he kept the other on the wheel.

"Nate. You're a very smart boy. Can you tell me why bad things happen to good people?"

The question caught me off guard. By now, I thought Mr. Garrison was quite bizarre. What kind of question was that? I had no idea. I thought maybe it was because God couldn't be everywhere, but I didn't know how religious Mr. Garrison was, and he had already infantilized me and my Jewishness the night before, and so I thought that any answer I could come up with might offend him.

"Is this the kind of question they will ask me at my interview for Exeter?" I asked. He looked at me incredulously.

"Don't joke around, Nate; this is a serious question. It is the kind of question that anyone can ask, but no one can answer."

I straightened my back in my seat and wondered why he would ask me a question if no one could answer it.

"Oh, well, sorry. I'm not really sure. Do you know?"

He shook his head.

"No, Nate, I don't know, but I wish I did," he said rather calmly, biting his lip at the end. And that was the end of our dialogue, for that car ride, at least.

When we got back, Mr. Garrison drifted off silently to wake his children while I sat alone by the kitchen and watched television. I greeted Jack and Arthur when they sauntered in, and I said hello to Rachel when she shuffled in later. I could not help but notice how fatigued everyone looked, especially Rachel, who had long lines underneath her eyes.

We sat quietly at the table while Mr. Garrison cooked eggs. He didn't look at anyone while he was cooking, except for fleeting moments when I noticed him watching me over the sizzling pans. He seemed nervous. I clasped my hands in my lap and tried to stare into space for a while. I thought silently to myself about whether or not Mr. Garrison carried on deeply philosophical conversations with Jack and Arthur. Then, for no reason at all, I looked at Rachel sitting next to me at the head of the table.

Our eyes locked instantaneously; her glare had pierced me to the point of shock. She had been looking at me all this time. Instead of looking away—like I usually would when I was embarrassed like this—I delved further into her expression for only an instant. There was a sadness in her eyes that persisted throughout this silent exchange, this quiet discourse where she did everything but utter the words, "Help me."

It was then that I knew. I did not quite understand what it was that I knew or how I could be so uncertain about what I perceived to be knowledge, but I knew that it happened. I knew it, but I couldn't believe it all at once, and for that, I would plague myself through silence.

Mr. Garrison coughed—perhaps he had noticed Rachel's unspoken inquiry—and asked us how we all liked our eggs. I refused to look at her again for the rest of the meal. I tried to stay quiet despite Arthur's attempts to turn the once somber atmosphere into a raucous one. I smiled at all their jokes and answered all of their questions politely, and for a brief amount of time, Mr. Garrison had stopped studying me.

We packed our bags immediately after breakfast. For a second, I thought Mr. Garrison might hold me back to talk to me again, but no, he had seemed to return to his usual self. I tried to comprehend all the recent events, and though I understood that somehow I had changed, I couldn't figure out exactly how or at what precise moment. Either that, or I had decided to try and forget that anything had changed at all.

"This weekend was awesome. Did you have fun?" Jack asked as he grabbed his backpack.

"It was awesome, man. I hope we do it again," I lied.

We packed ourselves into the car in the same way we had on the way to the Berkshires. Arthur sat up front and babbled with Mr. Garrison about his upcoming hockey practices. Jack and I talked nonsensically in the backseat, and Rachel, on the other side of us, would keep herself from the world, isolated with her headphones on, watching the trees whirl by endlessly.

But there was no mistaking the one difference between this ride and the last one. Mr. Garrison periodically observed me through his rearview mirror, pinning me down, transfixing me with fear; yes, too many years later, as I still try to forget, I am unable to rub the peculiarity of that sight from my memory.

LOVE'S THE GREATEST THING THAT WE HAVE —
(I'm waiting for that feeling)

A building. Almost a skyscraper, but it misses. The first hallway, a receptionist. An elevator. You go down. Right, and another hallway, this time more plain-looking. Older, less new style. No new style, actually. You're in the basement. Past the research room. Past the people on the computers; that's a head-hunting firm. The door to the stairs. Down the stairs. No, the elevator doesn't go down here. Through the next door. Ignore the rusty steel. The books are there for show. This isn't a library. It's dark. Head to the corner and go through the door. Two desks. They should still be there. At one, you see Clark. My boss. At the other, you've reached me, Jackson.

Tell us about what you do.

I sell Snow. Underground. Literally and figuratively.

Snow?

It's a drug. A nickname.

What kind of drug?

I don't know. It makes people feel displaced.

Interesting. Continue.

We're a telemarketing firm. We sell household devices. But Snow accounts for eighty percent of our profit. People say, "What happened to all the Snow?" You can't find it anywhere. Maybe abroad. But that's not allowed anymore. And they've cracked down on imports. We have the Snow. We're the only distributor in this region.

We don't all sell the Snow. One day, Clark moved me into

that room. He told me everything. The others, they sell household devices. As far as I know. Maybe some of them are on the in. Sometimes, I sell the devices, too, when I've failed. It's not easy.

You're always talking to men. They see where the call is coming from. Women don't dare pick up the phone. They don't want to die for treason. Not over a telemarketer. Not over me.

So, men don't need these devices, you're saying?

Men don't need most of these things. Most of them hang up. Especially if they're from an Outer Land. They don't have wives. Inner Land men tend to give more of their time. They also have more money. When you hint at the Snow, they will buy more often. The Outers are quicker to understand, but poorer. They also want it more. Either way, you do it slowly. You can't hurt the company. If the Government found us, who knows? Selling pleasure to people. It helps them cope with this situation. Even the Inners.

How do you sell? Give an example.

Start is standard. You're selling something. Not Snow, though. Not worth the risk. You introduce yourself. Let them hang up if they will. No pleasure for assholes. The few who talk, you mention it offhand. Weather sure is bleak. It's cold out here. But no snow, huh. I haven't seen snow for ages. Yes, it almost seems scarce. Scarce indeed. Wish I could produce some for you. Artificially. Artificially? You know. Yeah, I know, how much for three of those things you were talking about? Seven hundred. But are you an Inner or Outer? Inner. I'll have to industry mail it to you then, hidden. Right. Yes. Silence. He can't say sorry. It's treason. And they're listening.

So, you couldn't even ask him about women? Nothing about his wife?

No. I told you. They're listening. Always. All I know is that he has a wife. He has to. To reproduce. They tell us it's bad for us Outers. They tell us to love each other. Not women. I know better. I can't love men. I think we're unwanted. But the Inners who don't reproduce ... I don't know what happens. They don't come here. They've seen too much. That's my guess. For us, we just hope.

What about an Outer, then?

Less risk. They listen less. You name the price. Outers haggle. Then beg. Got two hundred now, can have the other hundred later. Promise. C'mon, man, I got nothing. I work, and I go home. I'm risking my life here, talking like this. Hope is the only thing I got. I want to help them. But I need the job. Because hope is my angle, too. I just didn't ask to sell Snow. Snow found me. It gives edge to my life. It is otherwise dull. I work overnight often. There is little to be had.

Why? Tell us about where you're from.

By that, I assume you mean where I reside.

Yes, currently, as you've been telling in your story.

Sheller. It's an Outer city. Two hours north of former New York City. You may know that name. It seems like any other place. All men. But no remnants of Inner society. We're like dogs. We can't watch sports. Women are in the crowd. Not even anything of Outer women cities. Even my mother. I have a photograph of her. You won't hurt me, right? It's illicit. Here it is. She looks strange. Is that what all women look like?

Yes, but like men, they have a variety of forms.

Yes, that's what I gather. I'm curious to see more of them.

You will. The war's over. We're here to free you. Things will change here, hopefully, or we'll take you back to Britain.

War? Is this why we work so hard lately? Industry is freedom, they say. They did mention a war. I didn't know if it was true. It is over?

Yes. But we're here now. We just want to know how this came to be. Your freedoms were taken from you very quickly. We found you shivering and clutching a note. You've never seen a real woman?

My last memory, it was so long ago. I was five. It feels like yesterday. I made fun of a girl in school. For being a girl. They told me I was impure. Toxic. But that was it. They took me away. They said there cannot be more like me anymore. My family, we never said goodbye. I don't understand. Why would they do that?

It's okay; we're just trying to help you. We are just trying to under-stand how this happened, in this country of all places. It was bombastic for a while, but we didn't think it would go this far. Go on, no more ques-tions, right, Robert? We don't have any more questions. Go ahead and tell your story.

* * *

I'm cold. I'm always cold. Darkness. It encapsulates the city. It gives you this feeling. Like the sun is not here. Somewhere else. Where souls are. I know it's there. But we're cold, like numb. Numb for repetition. We think we know another feeling. The feeling of not being like this. We all have seen illicit materials. But we don't discuss it. It's a silent understanding of that feeling.

The corner of the basement of a building. Behind dusty books. Rusty railings. Dirty square floor tiles. A part of Sheller. I was brought here at the age of five. Five years at a male orphan-age. I don't remember. Only in pieces. Individual moments, hazed.

Distortion. The distortion of my mind. Spent several years with a father, not my own. Haven't heard from them. They don't love me. Or they can't. My new father didn't either. He was a real lover. He had the gift of loving men. Lots of them in Sheller. Hence my theory. That we're unwanted. Because they can't reproduce. As for the non-lovers, we just feel unwanted. But we all did something wrong. That is what they say. Lovers are good people, fucked by the system. Sure, they can love. They can fuck. But they have to live here. With us. The unwanted. Without their gift. We can only love when we get that urge.

I went to a boys' school. I came home. I watched televi-sion. I learned to like other boys. More than just as friends. We played with each other. We experimented. I was confused. Many of us were. We learned this was good. It made us feel worse. We played sports. We tried to let it out. But we weren't close.

Parents constantly shifting. Friends changing with the parents. Always moving. No constancy. This is how things are. Still.

The building. My life for the past ten years. Routines make you forget. Not forget but blur. You blur. You wonder. Did this actually happen to me? You take a moment. You see it. But is it yours? What is it, anyway? And why not the rest of it? And are you making it all up?

I rise. I dress. I walk the streets. Other men like me. Some have learned to love. I have not. Just when I must. I cold call. All day. Clark sits by me. He knows something. He's seen women, I think. He won't say. He's in on something. He does—I don't know what. He listens. Sometimes, I call overnight. Clark gives me extra. If I'm lucky, Snow.

"Why don't people help us?" you said. I don't know. Many of us don't think we need help. Many only have memories of this place. We don't know anything. Texts banned. Archaic but useful texts. Illicit texts. We are hopeful. They make us hopeful. Promises. One day when you're ready. That's right. You might mate. You'll leave this place. Now, it's sinful. You don't deserve it. Yes, first you work. Work for those who help you. Think of all those in places just like this. But what about those who never worked? You don't ask. You can't ask. You can't understand. You can only do.

I had seen a woman two times here. First was obviously my mother. One day, I got a mysterious package. Inside was a man-lover magazine, nude men. I wondered why someone would send it. No return address. It had been scanned, approved by them. But they had missed the trick. The picture of my mother. Holding me in the hospital as a baby. It was carefully inserted. Where a leg should have been. A small note, too: "Can't risk you replying; this is the best I can do. Hopeful, others are too, your family silently. We are only following orders. Keep faith."

Family. I thought about having one.

Then, the other time, how I remember it so vividly. I have

forced myself to call upon it so as to never forget. I had a violation for potential espionage. False. I was brought into a government office. On the border of an Inner and an Outer Land. I had been escorted. From my place of residence. The building was amazing. Not a place I could ever imagine. Structures and images I have no words for. Color and beauty. It made me more scared. Powerless. I knew I was innocent. But didn't know why I was really there. Didn't know their motives. Thought maybe I was found out. Or that it was random hate. How could you know? Given the way things are. Things I disagree with. But I silently try to be good. Go about my business. Honor this great country. So, one day, I can love. But I don't tell anyone. Few know what I learned. Through the texts. They'd look down on me. They care little for women.

I was brought to a lobby. I thought it was over. Couldn't hurt to walk around. Since I was a dead man. You'd think it's where they watch the most. You'd be wrong. I left the lobby. Walked down a hall. There was music. I heard it. Faintly, then stronger. Stronger still as I grew close. The hall, thankfully empty still. The music growing. Anxiety rising. Feeling I could be caught any second. Killed instantly. Then I saw her.

She was obscured by an easel. But I could see the right side of her body. The nape of her neck. The music. It oozed in the background. She was painting a picture with her brush. So delicately. Her hair tucked around the left side of her body. I could only make the side of her face. But she seemed beautiful. Forbidden. But beautiful inherently. Not because she was forbidden. She seemed free. Careless of the people like myself who came in and out. Careless for my cause. I wanted her even more. I studied every moment. The light stroking of the bush on the paper. A light flick of her hair. The way she crossed her legs. These things were foreign to me. I wonder what kind of woman this is, if they come in different forms. She reminds me of my mother. Younger but so equally free.

A hand on my shoulder. A grunt. She turned her face; our

eyes met. Only an instant. Locked into my mind. Mouth askew.
A look of concern. Sympathy. So different. I wanted to touch.
But no. Dragged away. Commotion. Noise. Pain. A lengthy
interview. And then the worst part. Cleared, but a threat. If
you ever tell this story, you will be killed. So, I kept it inside.
The vision of her in my head.

"Why do you talk like this?" they say. Talk like what? Like
that, weirdly. I don't talk weird. This is how I always talk. Really?
This is how we all talk. Don't you even know that? Anger in my
voice, thought it was enough to kill me. They looked at me. The
same look the woman gave me. But not beautiful. One of them
said I was dumb. Not educated. One of them, he took out his
penis. He waved it at me. You like this, he said. He put it by my
face. You want to touch this penis. They laughed. I started to
touch. I thought he asked. He slapped me. Called me a name. I
walked free.

It comes back. The memory. All the time. Clark has his
way with me. At night, when all is still. Emptiness, except the
janitor. I get Snow. But I don't deserve it. I think of her when
it happens. He knows. He feels badly about it. He says someday he will make it up to me. It's not fair to Clark. He's trying
to love. I just don't know how. He's not a natural lover. He's
become one. Just the urges. We all get them. It's encouraged.
Just here. Not in the Inner Lands. You'd die there.

We go to the strip clubs. We watch the natural lovers dance.
We idolize them. We wish we had what they have. They pick us.
We oblige. We want to learn. Some of my friends, they've learned.
I can't learn. I want to try with a woman. Like the one I saw.

They make fun of me. When I can't learn. Or when I tell
them that. I try to keep it to myself.

In this town, phones are popular with teens. Makes them
feel displaced. Like Snow. We go to bars. It helps us sweat out
those angry bits of life. You know you face a beating sometimes. That stench. Puke, beer, and piss on your clothes. It's
what I do sometimes.

I forgot to say this, though. My other leisure. I have friends. Close ones. We watch television. We have clubs. We know we're together. It's these quiet friendships. That's how I feel. What's not said, it's better, those things. We feel we have the same feelings. We just can't say them. We pretend through the things we say. Like always enjoying the same movie. But sometimes I feel different. Like the extra sock in the laundry. But when I'm not that, I'm okay. Life is okay. They even call me Jack.

I tried to love. I had a boyfriend. Mark. I thought maybe he was handsome. Even to me. Objectively, yes, to everyone. I thought I was learning. He was assertive. He liked me dumb. He liked to teach. I received pleasure. But never love. I became assertive. I grew tired of him. I focus on my work.

Back to the building. Why did I tell you everything else? These things are dear to me. I think about change. How I would do it. I am a real person. I have feelings. How can I show that? It's what I ask. How can I find the return address? How can I find the woman from the office? How can I sell more Snow? How can I build wealth and prove my worth? Leave this place. This is my leisure. I enjoy these thoughts. But thoughts only. No writing. I take no risks.

So, things changed. At the building, like I said. My place of expectation. Where I know my day. Sure, different people are different. On the phone, I mean. Sure, I've been attacked coming home. By potential lovers. Only sometimes. But I know what to expect in general.

I was selling lots of Snow. Good day for me. Clark could hear. I even learned a thing or two. About women. Sometimes, you learn. On the phone. When an Inner says something. By mistake. They know where the call is from. That's why women don't pick up. One Inner, though. Talked about his wife's cooking. Now I knew why. The correlation of my sales. Mostly to Inners. For their wives' cooking. Made me wonder about them.

At night, Clark said, do an overnight. I agreed. Clark puts the list on my desk. Tattered, used, maybe. A phone number circled toward the end. When you get there, you call forever, he says. Let it ring until someone answers. Very important. Don't care if it takes three days. Lot on the line here. You understand? Yes, I understand. And I wonder. Why never before? But Clark leaves. After looking me in the eye. Stronger than ever.

Hesitating, looking down, putting his hand on the desk, concerned. Touching my shoulder. Squeezing. Then leaving.

Time passes. I call East Coast. Then, Midwest. Then, West Coast. It's late. Janitor sweeps dust out the door. Pops his head in. Waves to me. Good man. Been here since before me. Says goodnight. I nod because I'm on a call. Selling a portable oven. No Snow. Failure and success. Intermingled. Two things in one. Money is money. Success, really. He's never done Snow. The guy on the phone with me. I can tell.

I gorge on the energy pills. This is it. The last push. It's 1 AM. Calling known buyers now. The circled number looms. I keep wondering. What is it; what is it? I am almost rushing. This is so new. Exciting, for the building. Even for my friends. After the easy sales, the packaging slips, the hidden containers to pass through security, it comes.

I dial. Ring. Over and over. Thirty seconds. More ringing. 1 minute. I look at my watch. Two minutes. Wonder if Clark is joking. But can't take risks. Five minutes. I stare into space. The hallway out my door. It's dark. I leave it open overnight. The eerie silence. I wonder who occupies it. And who doesn't. Who makes those sounds? Those creaks. It's not my imagination.

Ten minutes. I think of hanging up again. I start to do it. But I can't. I remember the squeeze. On my shoulder. So, I just put down the phone. I stretch. I pick it up. Still ringing. I lean back. I think. All different kinds of things. Slowly, slowly. Never before, but yes, now. I fall asleep. Softly, quietly. The darkness gathering. The corner of a basement in a building. All in a dark, empty city. Sheller asleep. And finally, me too.

I jolt awake. It's been two hours. Panic. Fidgeting a lot. My soul burning. No one knows. I am safe here. And the phone still rings. 3:22 AM. Clark will be back in a few hours. I can show him then. It keeps ringing. 3:37 AM. Playing with elastics. Thinking of Lenny. My friend. We are supposed to see a film. About the rise of Sheller. An industrial capital of our fine country.

3:47 AM. I keep waiting. This must be a joke. But Clark, I never know with him. It's ambiguous. Like his sex.

It happens in the tiniest increments of time. The pause. No ring. I kick myself up.

Breathing heavy. The sound of an answer. A short breath. And then, a voice. A female voice. "Hello?"

Here comes that panic attack. My heart stops. And then it starts. I think of it all. Wanting desperately to reply. Is this a test? Is Clark testing me? Are they listening? But I can't think. Not properly. I react. "Hi."

"I've been waiting for you," it says quickly. Not stirred by my silence. It's patient. The voice is patient. It reminds me of the painting girl. I imagine her. She seemed patient. She was not mad at me. Why is she waiting for me? This must be a wrong number.

"I must have the wrong number. Please don't hurt me." I start to hang up. But I can't. She is already speaking.

"No, you have the right number. Don't be scared. We're fine here."

Maybe it's not a woman. But why are we fine here? Why say that?

"Are you a woman?"

I hate myself. Why did I say that? I am going to die. It's what I think. I've been so good. Even when they brought me in. I didn't mean to be bad. But I was a dead man walking. And I walked. Maybe I can walk again.

"Yes, I am, Jackson. I am a woman."

She knows my name. No one ever knows my name. I have to say it. But she knows it. What is Clark up to? This is a fix. I knew I didn't trust Clark. He uses me. He hides things. What are the creaking noises? Are they coming to get me now? They must be. Abducting me. I deserve it for sinning.

"Oh." It's all I can think to say. I'm too scared. "Sure is late ... and cold."

Yes, yes, it is.

"Yes ... yes, it is."

Her breath. Muffled on the phone. I try to picture her. Like the other woman.

Curvy lips. Soft skin. Long hair, like silk. My eyes are closed. I don't care if they take me. I try not to think. Clark is powerful. Maybe he has these connections. Maybe I just be quiet. Go with it.

"Are you lonely, Jackson?"

Lonely ... what is lonely? I don't know "lonely." I feel weird sometimes, yes. But always included. I have friends. I have things to occupy my mind. But lonely. I feel lonely. Only when I think of the photograph. Or the mental image of her. The feeling of potential. Yes, lonely. I've learned to never say it. Now I do.

"Yes."

I want to cry. Why is this happening to me? I want to be home. I also want to stay here. But as a ghost. Not as me. I want to watch from afar. Safely. From the darkness. From the creaking.

"I know you are. I am, too." An Outer?

"Are you an Outer, too?"

"No." Quick again. Defiantly. "I am what I am."

Confusion. But this is not my world. She is from somewhere else. I am from here. I am what I am. It makes more sense to me. Kind of.

"I see."

A pause, a breath. My heart fluttering.

"I need you to come meet me."

My heart drops. Into my stomach. I never leave in the middle. I check the clock. 3:53 AM. Let alone to see a woman. And where. It is all too confusing. I have come this far. So, I ask. "How much Snow?"

No surprise. Thankfully. I don't want to die. Or get arrested.

"No Snow. Just you. I am your mother's only hope."

My mother. It makes me want to cry. I don't understand what she means. Before I can ask, she speaks again.

"How much time do we have?"

I want to ask what this is. Am I going to die? Is this a test? Why are you doing this? How do you know my name? But I've sat here ten years. Never this. Not even the pictures change. The silence, the same. The creaking, louder now, the same. I don't want to ruin it. I don't want to die. But I feel safe. Clark could be helping me. He wanted me to talk to her. Clark knows. Clark knows my loneliness. When I lie limp for him. When I close my eyes when he does it to me. He knows. He feels it. I feel it in him, too.

"Not long. The sun will rise." No hesitation. "Meet me at East Shamrock and Albany; down past the baker shop, there is a small alleyway, no monitors. Be there within ten minutes. I don't take chances."

A click. She is gone. Ten minutes. The place, it is not that close. And I don't even know. My mind, it's muddled. It feels like mud. Clogged. Dirtied. Sullied by these thoughts. I'll be seen. They're watching. She'll be caught. I'll get caught. Or I already have been. It's too late. I leave.

It's dark. I'm cold. The night yearns. I'm lost inside. The creaking grows. Are they coming? I don't know yet. The pipes drip. The books, they're there. I feel him lurking. In the shadows of the shelves. Yes, he watches me. Late at night. I quicken my pace. The creaking grows. I approach the door. It presses on my ears. The lurker. Is he in my mind? I open the door. Rats. On the pipes. I am free. He is the trouble of my mind. He is not real. Though I swear I see his eyes in the darkness. Pleasuring himself. While I call. From the distance. But is he real? Not tonight.

Up the stairs. Past the computers. Past the research room. Left. The elevator. I ascend. I am rising. But I have no time. I burst through the lobby and out the door. Avoid suspicion. Walk briskly. You're wary of criminals. That's right. Nothing suspicious. You can make it in time. You will make it. You have eight minutes.

The city sleeps, but it feels awake. Not because I am seen. Because it's begging. Always begging for something. I don't know what. Something. It is never at rest. And now I am not either. I am looking everywhere. Ahead, behind. Above, below. Side to side. Everywhere, awaiting the end. I want to think of the things. The ones that are my leisure. Is this a part of my plan? But I can't. It's all too fast. I'm running ahead of myself. I'm not myself. I am the ghost I wanted to be.

A minute left. I can see it. The sight of it. It makes me stop. I ask myself, am I ready? I think about Lenny. Clark. The woman in the photo. Holding the baby me. Will I see them again. Will I sacrifice one to see the other? Is this my bridge? Is this my fate? Is this nothing at all? An experience. A temptation.

I linger at the alley. I press my ear. No sound. I try to peek in. Nothing. I turn the corner. I enter the abyss. It's dark. Darker than the city. I can feel myself losing feeling. I barely breathe. I send out whispers to the world. Hear me, please. I feel with my arms.

Along the brick walls. It gets lighter. Still dark, but lighter. My breath escapes me. Dimly lit. There she is.

She is beautiful. Like my mother. A body so unlike ours. One I didn't understand. She smiles at me. I gape. I am horrified. I am happy. I am something I can't describe. I am really the ghost. I can feel myself leaving my body. But I have not been killed yet.

She walks to me.

"I thought you wouldn't make it." And then a touch. It tingles. On my shoulder. Different than Clark's touch. I look at her hand. I feel it. My face, the same. I feel her eyes. I know, then. Why we are separate. They are more powerful. They are dangerous. They have powers we don't. But I feel safe. She knows me.

"I've been watching you for some time, Jack."

I look at her. Finally. I could not do it. Now I have to. I have grown scared. The shadows, they scare me. Am I being watched? Is this going to end? Has Clark ended me? Is it a test? I'm committing treason. She is one of them. After all this. She sees it. She has powers.

"Don't be scared, Jack. I came a long way to give you hope. To give us a legacy."

I cry. The sobs, they are foreign to me. It has been so long since crying. "Help me, please."

She takes the hand off my shoulder. Presses my face onto her own shoulder. I correct myself.

"Or just kill me."

I'm not suicidal. Life is okay. I'm just conscious. Aware of what she may do. Aware that asking for help is treason. But seeing her, it makes me crave death. Like life is fulfilled. Like this is all I get. Like it makes an escape. Like the stairs from my desk. The ones that go to the elevator. To the lobby and out.

"We don't have much time," she whispers. And then, "I love you," as she kisses me.

The forbidden word. Love. There is no love. We don't know love yet. That's what they say. The texts. I shiver. The kiss is warm. Different than Clark's. He rarely does it. Different than the other times. The times I was attacked.

I try to kiss back. There is nothing now. Nothing but me. The consequences, they are nothing too. This is life. If life is those thoughts. Those thoughts of leisure. Then this is the climax. This I need to savor.

She unbuttons my pants. I am aroused. A rare feat. She is an Inner. I see the mark.

When she takes off her shirt, it's there. But also, her breasts. Soon, we are naked, except for my shirt. And I slip inside. She is warm. She protects me from the city. The cold. The shadows. The begging.

Through breaths, I ask, "How do you know me?" I feel better. I can talk. I am invincible.

She mumbles in whispers. Moaning. But I can't hear. And I don't want to ask again. I imagine she says, "I am your sister." Yes, she could have. Out of breath. I keep thrusting. My sister. Do I have a sister? How can one know? Is she lying? She is mysterious. The reply seems typical. Something to keep me away. To remind me. She is the dominant one. The one with the powers. I am still me. No longer the ghost. I re-enter my body, confused. She pulls me close. Then, suddenly, pure ecstasy. Release inside of her as I collapse. She sighs. For a moment, I feel divine. Not a ghost, but above. I can see the city. I look down on it. It's just the city. Not anything I've made it out to be. Just the city. Small and stupid. Beneath me. Full of unprivileged. But I am not one of them.

I feel connected. We are one. She sighs repeatedly. The ecstasy leaves my body, enters hers. It's electrical. I feel the tingling. I assume her powers. We are one. Then our eyes lock.

As she withdraws, I feel like a knife has come out of me. Quickly, she runs away. Hope escapes me. I lurch. Have I been betrayed? Have I been tested for treason? Has Clark set this up? Did he know all along? What is real after all this? I look down. No blood. But I am in pain. I look up to show my pain. But she is gone.

And I know I am going to die. She has powers, and I feel weak. I crawl home, slowly. Weaker and weaker. Betrayed. But not concerned. More aware of my loss. She is gone. I try to re-capture it in my head. But it's already a haze. I reach my apartment. I barely reach the keyhole. I slide it in, just enough energy left. I climb the stairs. Tears everywhere. Elbows, then legs. I'm weak from loss. The feeling of detachment. I crawl into my bed to sleep forever. My mind escapes itself. I drift away. Weaker and weaker. I await death. But even though I sleep, I awake. Feeling healthy again. Forlorn.

Or, she wasn't there. She never was. I wanted her to be there. I can't be sure. Maybe we never spoke. Maybe she is just as real as the lurker. I can't know. I can't know anything. It's always a haze. I tried to piece it together. As I crawled home. Was she there? Will I see her again? Did I imagine my betrayal? Was I scared? Did I require the betrayal in my mind? How can I see her again, even if she is in my mind? Or was she never there at all?

Love's the greatest thing that we have. I'm waiting for

that feeling. But I think I know what it's like. I try to re-live it. Whenever I can, I do. In my mind. It's not a safe place. It's a frustrated place. It wants to understand. It wants to know. But sometimes, I think I do know. Not just because she is so vivid. Like the painting woman. Like my mother. I keep the shirt hanging. In my room. The bloodless shirt. And a note. I woke up with it. Clenched in my hand. It tells me when we'll meet again.

THIS IS THE STORY THAT I WROTE FOR THIS WEEK —

"If I could replace any of my body parts with animal parts, I think I would replace my feet with monkey feet so that I could still be me and also be one-of-a-kind like a praying mantis."

This is the opening line to the short story I wrote for my creative writing class this past week. Trivial? Maybe. Brilliant? Absolutely. I'll let you in on my little secret in a moment.

By now, I have come close to mastering the art known as Creative Writing. I'm in my third class in college, which qualifies me as "Advanced." Obviously, I understand that many of my classmates share this qualification; however, I have scrounged around for bits of knowledge that they have not. And because of that, I plan on writing a book sometime in the near future.

Creative writing classes are pretty laid-back. Students write stories and send them out to the class to be edited and appraised. In other words, they allow their stories to be torn to shreds, effectively putting any remaining self-confidence in jeopardy. The actual degradation occurs in class. This is called a workshop. Up until the age of eighteen, my greatest fear was snakes. Now, it's workshops.

Perhaps I am a little biased about workshops, but I will try to explain them as objectively as possible. There are usually a few student works to discuss, so the teacher will arbitrarily choose one to begin with. Then, the analysis begins. At first, it seems pleasant. People will say nice things about the story—even if they hate it—because otherwise, they would be rude. I'm not fooled by these pleasantries. The criticism kicks in subtly.

"I wonder how objective the narrator is in the scene describing the terrorist ..."

Eventually, it becomes outright and daring.

"Let's be serious. The scene with the urgent telephone call makes NO sense. This story is supposed to take place in the 1700s! There were no phones back then."

In case you're wondering, these are actual responses to stories I wrote in my first creative writing class. The one about the 1700s was a silly mistake. I'm still not sure about the feedback with the terrorist, though—I think terrorists are objectively pretty bad, but we will talk about some of my classmates later on.

The whole thing is pretentious. We go into class in this haughty manner, pencils fastened to our ears, legs crossed, basically having a dick-waving contest for the teacher dropping names of famous authors or their works for extra kudos when rendering feedback. It's as if we have the notion that our works will eventually be published as part of a novel, such that we seek the ideas of others so that we can all go home and write our stupid novels. And none of us are even old enough to buy a beer.

But I have pined nonetheless to succeed in these classes because I enjoy writing. But what is not fair is how hard I have had to work to get to where I am now. Do you know how hard it is to be a straight white male these days and be taken seriously? You should try it sometime. You're canceled before you even start typing. And to make matters worse, coming up with story ideas is tough. I try to riff off of current events, but then I get worried people will think I'm really not creative. And it's a Creative Writing class.

So, it's hard to write short stories. For me, at least. Not for that jerk who seems to resurface in all my different classes—albeit not the same person—who writes based on everyday experiences. For this guy, writing is easy. He takes some funny or important real-life event and writes about it as if it's fiction. I always get nervous about doing that because sometimes I write really dark and weird shit, and I don't want anyone to think it's based on a true story.

However, I have picked up on the types of things that do make a successful story.

Generally, they need to be deep, or at least imply some greater outlook on life.

Depressing stories usually fit here. Something else I noticed is that random, descriptive references to things make a story seem better than it really is. The more random something is, the more impressed people are by it. Like when one of my class-mates alluded to a character wearing a green-striped tie and proceeded to write two paragraphs about the tie, never to return to this character at all in the story—everyone was impressed by the vivid description. I guess that brings me back to the open-ing line of *my* story that revolved around exchanging human feet for monkey feet. You gotta admit it—when you read that line, you suspected I had written a good story.

More recently, I have found that everyone loves a compel-ling victim. One of my stories about a Navajo descendant who buys a house on land that once belonged to his tribe was a mas-sive hit in one of my recent classes. You just need to have the right victim. When I wrote about poor white people in West Virginia who were dying of cancer years after exposure in the coal mines, I was lambasted by my classmates for co-opting white supremacy through my words. I used it as a data point to refine my focus on which victims matter and which ones do not. You need to have a growth mindset in this business: treat all the criticism as an opportunity to do better.

I'll give you one final and very much related example, for I don't want to give away all my secrets. Issues pertaining to diversity are golden. If you write passionately about anyone or anything that has been discriminated against unjustly, not only will everybody find you to be a bold, courageous hero and a champion of what is right in the world, no one will ever have the guts to criticize you. Never. To emphasize this point in my story, I made sure to include a character who is a gay, black, female Jew who is also Muslim. Unless someone is will-ing to go against the sexuality, race, sex, or religion card, I feel like she is pretty much untouchable.

Plot twist: turns out she (they?) are actually non-binary as you get further along in the story, so add "transphobia" to the mixed bag of "isms" you might commit by criticizing the character or the story. It forces the reader to reconcile with their own biases and assumptions and raises serious questions about the reliability (and possible transphobia) of the narrator who had misgendered them. It also raises questions about whether or not they are still even gay. My (possibly) gay, black, transgender Jew? There is a small bit in there about how they are not recognized as a human being in the world for the intersectionality of these deeply unique traits that absolutely define their character, but it turns out they are not core to the story. You could say they did not get in there based on merit, but more so out of fear of criticism from my classmates.

Well, that was a pretty hefty introduction to the world of creative writing. I would like to actually tell you about the intense experience I had in work-shopping this piece. I am used to having my pieces work-shopped. Each time, my heart beats a little faster, I have some noticeable trepidation, and I pray that everyone will like my story. In the past, I knew some of my stories were bound to fail, and I was eager to learn. But this one is a gem. My intersectional character isn't even the half of it, trust me. It is the first one I have written with my completely new perspective on creative writing, and I was actually excited about the fact that my classmates would be reading it.

Basically, I thought it would go straight to the bookstore. You can imagine that I was pretty nervous about class this time around because I was relying so heavily on the success of this piece. If it failed ... I didn't know if I could keep writing. When considering that it was the most enjoyable activity for me since becoming a college student, the situation becomes magnified. Literally life or death for me.

I showed up to class that day just like it was any other day. I played it cool that I had written a story for that day, but deep down I was hoping for glints of optimism from everyone's eyes. My professor greeted me cheerfully, which, at the very least, was not a bad thing. He had written many books and was pretty famous, so if he liked my story, it meant that I was destined for stardom. Standing in my way, however, were the opinions of my peers who could ultimately sway him. Perhaps he loved my piece, I thought, and my classmates would say such awful things about it that he had never considered that he would just spit at it and kick me out of class.

Some of my other classmates trickled in and took their seats. A couple talked amongst themselves, one brown-nosed to the professor about a story she had read over the weekend, and the rest of us just pulled out our notebooks and stared into space for a while. I think I was shaking uncontrollably, but it's a nervous tic that I cannot control. People usually have to hit me to make me even realize what I am doing when that happens.

"So," my professor said. "Let's take a look at Jeff's piece, 'Mantis.' Very interesting title. Quite perplexing read ..." His lip curled as he said this.

I thought to myself, *What the hell does that mean?*

"Definitely refreshing, vibrant, new—spicier than your past works, Jeff. What did you all think of this? Try to start with positives, if you can."

If you can?

I hid a smile and pulled out a pencil, opening my notebook so I was ready to take notes based on my classmates' opinions. I was hoping to have very little to write in the notebook. I wanted this piece to be perfect.

There was dead silence. No one would raise their hands to say anything positive about my story. Panic set in. My heart was racing. I did not even look up at everyone; I was so embarrassed.

"I liked it."

Ella, the cute girl next to me, had blurted out her approval of my story. I could always count on her for encouragement. She liked my stories for some reason, never keen to elaborate on why. I had the inkling that maybe she just liked me; indeed,

I got that vibe often. She was always smiling at me. Despite this, I never had the nerve to ask her out. What if I ended up hating one of her stories? I just think it wouldn't work out.

After bringing about a silence even more awkward than the first, she continued.

"The characters were real in this story. There were no cli-chés or artsy-fartsy exaggerations. The dialogue was believ-able. Crude sometimes, maybe, but that's how we talk. I dunno, it just seemed to work for me."

I was relieved. She had something nice to say about some-thing new I had incorporated into this story. I was destined for greatness, after all.

My professor gave her a slight nod and folded his arms. Leaning back in his chair, he peered through his thin-rimmed glasses and turned his head back and forth to look at other students. Seeing a hand in the corner, he motioned for someone to speak without even opening his mouth. I looked up from my notebook.

Shit.

It was the bitchy feminist girl who always sat in the back and groaned, complaining about the slightest of details, not the least of which was the lack of empowerment of women. I had seen so many people like this girl on social media that, honestly, I just knew by looking at her that she was one and the same.

She's gonna say it. I can't believe she's going to say it. I should've known she would be so angry about Linda when I wrote the story. She hates men.

"I thought the description of Linda was a little unjust. You called her a 'slut' on page four, even insisting that she would not go out on the weekends when she was on her period because she could not have sex on those days. I don't see how realistic this description can possibly be when considering that in our society, men tend to be more sexually driven than women. I found it offensive that you would make a character who doesn't go out when she is menstruating *just* because she can't have sex.

It's as if you are saying that hinders her somehow."

I knew it.

I nodded my head profusely, grabbed the pencil from my left ear, and started scribbling away in my notebook.

"Girl in corner is still a fucking cunt," I wrote, adding a few more scribbles for good measure and my own amusement. I looked up at her and smiled. She glared back at me.

My professor coughed and scratched the few hairs on his balding head, giving me a concerned look at the same time. I looked around the room with a half-smile as if I were eager for more rampant criticisms like those of my nemesis, the bitchy feminist.

"What do you think of that assessment, Walter?" My professor turned his head to the boy sitting across from me, who I like to refer to as "slit-my-wrists-guy." He writes really depressing stories about loneliness and killing and all kinds of things that really make me think that this class is much sadder than the Holocaust class I took last semester. Not to mention the fact that he carries this attitude into class with him. Sometimes, I want to tell him that he missed the sign-ups for drama class and was accidentally placed in creative writing, but I'm not that mean. In a perfect world, I would, though, because he really pisses me off.

Slit-my-wrists-guy pulled his gray hoodie down and leaned forward to cup his arms over his notebook. He then de-clasped his hands to rub one of the dark circles under his eyes before re-clasping them and looking me straight in the eyes. He sighed, then spoke.

"Well, to be honest, I think you lose some of your 'scholarly tone' with your crude humor. That applies to some other lines in the story, like page six with the praying mantis. Tom describes it as follows: 'I saw a praying mantis today for the first time in my life. I thought it was a really big deal, so I took a picture of it. But then it started doing all this weird *praying mantis shit*, bobbing back and forth, so I ran away.' After his friends tell him praying mantises are not that rare, he says, 'Fuck you, guys, you ruined my day.' Realistic or not, what kind of audience do you want this to appeal to? Furthermore, your realism is really idealism. I found the ending to be void of happiness or at least a false aspiration for it."

"Well, is that necessarily bad, Walter?" My professor was coming to my defense. I gave him a surprised look, but his attention was fixed on slit-my-wrists-guy. Slit-my-wrists-guy did not even hesitate.

"Not at all. But this Linda character is so flawed in the story that your intention of a subtly happy ending comes across as quite sad because the reader knows, or at least thinks, that she will not live happily ever after."

"Hm," said my professor, considering slit-my-wrists-guy's idea. *No way. He did not just convince the professor that my story is bad.*

"I suppose that makes a lot of sense, Walter. It does change the outlook of the story. Then again, I don't know if it matters what Jeff wanted to do. The ending could be powerful any way you look at it. Besides, it is very rare for a praying mantis to have wings, and you need to remember that the praying mantis in this story does have them."

I breathed a sigh of relief, but I was still anxious. I had just dodged a bullet. I wanted to wink at slit-my-wrists-guy, but I wasn't completely sure I had won the war just yet (perhaps the battle), so I kept up my fake curious emotion as if I was eager for more valid criticisms. Deep down, I knew things were going well so far, aside from the failed cancellation attempt.

I'm a superstitious guy. I have feelings that people are due to succeed when they are failing, and vice-versa. The sick feeling I had in my stomach was progressively growing with all the positive or refuted negative comments because I knew the momentum would not last. So, despite my positive feelings, I felt like throwing up when the bitchy feminist raised her hand with her trademark bitchy frown from the corner.

Not again. What else can she possibly say that she hasn't already? I hate her.

"Back to the point about Linda's menstruation ..."

You've got to be kidding me.

"If she really is as 'slutty' as you intend her to be, wouldn't she just go out and fuck on her period anyway?"

Wow.

I was in love. Not because I thought this was at all a good idea; in fact, I found it repulsive. But it was the most daring thing I had ever heard anyone say in a classroom. I couldn't believe she used the word "fuck" in class! Not to mention what she was implying with her statement. Ella was no longer my favorite girl in the class—the bitchy feminist had some balls.

The whole class was in awe, but no one had the nerve to laugh. I think the professor was shocked as well. But it is an arts class. You can pretty much say anything you want and get away with it because you're being artistic. Somehow.

I don't think two seconds passed before the stoner guy chimed in from the end of my side of the table. "Yeah, I was thinking that too. Because I tried that once with a girl, and it wasn't so bad. And you really went out of your way to portray Linda's promiscuity."

What's going on here? Am I dreaming? Is this happening? And is my story really being criticized solely for Linda's menstrual cycle?

I looked around the room to see if anyone was as mortified as I was. No one, except Ella, had jaws dropped as far as mine. I quickly put myself back together and scribbled down some thoughts in my notebook.

"*Stoner guy got high before class again, has really fucked up ideas. Consider changing idea about Linda's menstruation. Maybe delete it entirely. Too much weird shit to worry about.*"

"I actually had a few suggestions myself."

Ah, Steven. It was inevitable that he would come up with something to dash my hopes. He was the best writer in the class, and he intimidated me. I could never seem to affect him emotionally with my stories; he would sit there stoically, unfazed by anything I wrote, and simply make me feel inferior. Even when I offered help to my classmates in their workshops, he would occasionally refute my points. He epitomizes smart-ass.

What do you have this time, Steven?

"Basically, the voice of the narrator is all off. He should be more objective; I don't think you planned on giving an omniscient view from Tom's perspective. The story would benefit from seeing the story from all angles because there is a lot going on, and I feel that it's limited from the viewpoint you've given. Secondly, some of your ideas are outright disgusting. I vomited a little in my mouth when I read this. My tertiary point would be that you could incorporate more random references and go to hell because you are an awful person."

Okay, he didn't say that last part, but you get the gist of it. He didn't really like my story. I tried my best not to reach across the table and strangle him to death. Instead, I pointed my pencil in his direction as if he had awakened me to newfound insights. I then wrote some things down in my notebook.

"Steven continues to like big words. Probably compensating for small penis."

Fortunately, no one seemed to take too kindly to his words. Even my professor had a furrowed brow and a questioning look. So, I guess I came across as a pretty open guy, tipping my pencil in Steven's direction and pretending to heed his advice. Even the bitchy feminist crossed her arms and stared at her lap.

Finally. Other people feel awkward about what's going on in this class right now.

One of Ella's friends, Emily, decided to jump into the conversation. I actually like Emily. I'd like her more than Ella, but Emily has a boyfriend, so she loses some major brownie points for that.

"This story was beautiful," she said. "Yeah, I was very moved by it. I would like to go back to the ending. I know Walter discussed it, but I had a very different take on it. We are all forgetting how this story comes full circle. The monkey feet at the beginning are not trivial. When Linda decides that she would want praying mantis wings at the end so that she can fly away, we see how brave she really is. Yeah, she has problems, but she's much smarter than Tom and all the other characters. You know, female praying mantises eat their male counterparts. This story wasn't sexist at all. I think Jeff made some points that he wanted us to pick up on. Finally, like our professor noted, not all praying mantises grow wings. For Linda to acquire wings and fly away would make her a very special character. And I don't know if Walter is right about the mood of the ending. It's pretty sad that she feels the way she does, regardless of what her future will hold."

God bless you, Emily. God bless you. Thank you for understanding that I have been a champion for women all this time.

"Thanks, Emily," I blurted. My cheeks must have been red. You're not supposed to address people's comments until after they are done discussing your piece. But I was so flattered that I had *moved* her. That's why I want to be an acclaimed writer. The power to make people feel a certain way is, to me, indescribable in a very good way.

"That's an interesting take on the piece, Emily," said the professor. I hated how objective he was. Why couldn't he just either take my piece and throw it in his fireplace or sign me up with a publisher? This purgatory of work-shopping was frustrating but hopefully worthwhile nonetheless.

A few more people made comments. Someone else in the class made a point about my gay, non-binary, black, Jew/Muslim character and how it was racially insensitive, but I found that inherently racist because if that was racist, then it should have also been sexist, homophobic, Islamophobic, and anti-Semitic. Then, there was an argument amongst everyone in the class accusing my accuser of being transphobic for misgendering the character and whether the character could be religiously non-binary as well. I wrote in my notebook, "*Black people don't like when white people try to write about black people.*"

Other than that, everything else was pretty minor. I felt

pretty good, and the best part was that I could see that Steven was angry about my success. He looked like he had a bad case of indigestion. Man, did he look uncomfortable.

Everyone proceeded to hand me their individual comments, and I accepted them graciously. When the professor asked me if I had anything to say, I declined. I sat back and relaxed while my classmates ripped on the bitchy feminist's story about Margaret Sanger. Then we talked about Emily's piece, which I really liked. I made sure to reciprocate by saying very nice things and coming to her defense every time Steven tried to bring her down. I almost came to blows with slit-your-wrists-guy about how depressing the story was because it was probably one of the happiest stories I had ever read. I got my revenge when we reviewed his piece (about a widow who commits suicide) by telling him that, obviously, there were no telephones in the eighteenth century. What an idiot.

Class ended. Everyone put their notebooks in their bags and started to file out of the classroom, but I hung behind. My professor took his glasses off, gave me a quick smile, and pushed his chair back so he could stand. As he approached his desk, I started putting my things together. Once I was sure that everyone was gone for good, I spoke to him.

"So ... Professor Green. Not to be weird or anything, but did you think my story was any good? Or at least an improvement?"

He squinted at me cautiously, then reached for his glasses and sat down at his desk.

"Why don't you take a seat over here, Jeff?"

This can't be good.

I walked very deliberately and sat down in the chair he had pointed out to me by his side.

"Jeff..."

Yes?

"Do you really think that Jackie is a fucking cunt?"

This isn't happening. Did he really just say that?

"I bet you're thinking I didn't just say that," he chuckled nervously.

How can he read my thoughts?

"But don't worry, I can't read thoughts or anything."

Right.

"Uhh ... what are you talking about?"

"Jeff, I sit right next to you in class. I can see your notes—"

Shit.

"... And you don't seem to be getting much from your classmates."

I put my head down on my chest and looked squarely at my feet. "Yes. I guess I do feel that way about her."

"Interesting" was all he had to say. It was as if I was speaking to a therapist.

Where was this going? After what seemed like an interminable silence, he spoke again.

"Well, Jeff, I suppose if I were you, I'd feel the same way. But I'm not you, am I?"

Evidently. Get on with your point.

"Okay, I can see you are confused about where I am going with this. Basically, my experience has taught me that accepting the criticism of others is the most helpful thing for a writer. You can't expect that everything you write will be perfect. I suppose it's natural to feel that way because it's yours and you have an emotional attachment to it. But stereotyping others and rejecting their advice will limit your success."

Oh.

"To answer your question though, Jeff, yes, I thoroughly enjoyed your story. It is better than many of the works of my colleagues. I could see you becoming a writer and maybe publishing what you have here, with a little more work ... one day."

I blushed, but this had little to do with the bitchy feminist ... Jackie. I was starting to wonder if stereotyping her was fair or productive. And I didn't really care anymore that he really liked my story or that my dreams might come true. I sensed that there was a catch coming, and my intuition was correct.

"But," he added, "you don't write with the correct intention. Your intent is to seek approval and not to embrace the journey associated with growth. What you fail to see in someone like Jackie is that she holds the key to making you successful because she has unique insight into where your messaging may be weak or vulnerable. Once you understand her perspective, you can then take on the challenge of incorporating her comments without compromising the original, contrarian message of your story."

I felt enlightened and dumb at the same time. It made so much sense. But he wasn't done yet.

"In any event, Jackie may not be as colorful as you, but she writes about things she is truly passionate about. Whether or not you agree with her, she believes in something, and she wants to help you see it, too. She wants to affect her readers and make them see the world the way she does. You ..." he trailed off.

"What do I do?"

He took a deep breath.

"You find cute ploys to make your story engaging. They're funny sometimes, and yes, the reader can be fooled into thinking it is a great work. And sure, you could sell it and make some money, maybe, but how would you feel about that? Write from your heart, Jeff; that's all I can say. If you'll excuse me, however, I have a meeting to make. I need to review a story from another student before she sets off for Prague."

And that was all I was left with. Prague. I felt insignificant. At the same time, I knew I was blessed with powerful advice; I was lucky. You might call it bittersweet, but somehow, I knew that Professor Green liked me and wanted me to succeed.

When I got back to my room, I tore up "Mantis" and threw it in the garbage. It was like losing a part of me that I didn't need anymore, like my wisdom teeth. It hurts a little at first, but then you realize you're better off. I sat down at the computer to start my next piece. This one isn't going to my classmates, though; I'm writing it just for fun. It's a lot different from my past works, too. I know I said that about the last one, but I really mean it this time. I know now that it takes several evolutionary stages to become the writer I want to be. This time, it's a creative non-fiction piece, and you're reading it right now.

KICKING STONES —

These days, I can't help thinking about Ravenstown because I tried so hard to just put it away, but now, I only feel guilty. Being in college kept me distracted for a while, but I know deep down that this feeling of guilt only got bigger and bigger once I got there in the first place. I was just trying to suppress it and imagine that everything I had done was logical, like any other person would do the same. I guess that may be true, that I just did what I had to do, but I still feel awful, and I can't really explain why, and none of my friends here at school would really understand, so maybe you will.

I'm going back to Ravenstown to honor my childhood friend. My Aunt Sally called me on the dorm phone yesterday, and I knew it was going to be bad news because it was not my birthday. I've been through a lot, but it was the first time some-one ever called me on the phone to tell me that someone died. I think it was weird for her because she felt even guiltier than I did that I lost touch with him, and I know she only got the news from my mother, who I haven't spoken to either.

I didn't really know what to say because I was only in the process of moving on with my life, so hearing about it just brought me back to another time and place, and it almost made me feel a bit nostalgic. In some ways, my friends had already died years ago, and I would just wonder about them from time to time and whether or not they were even still out there. This made them feel real again. I didn't want to believe it, so I looked up the obituary online.

ATEKA 'TEK' ALI, 20

Ateka "Tek" Ali, 20, of Ravenstown, Ohio, died on October 14, 2004, in a train accident.

No service will be held. Friends of Mr. Ali are currently arranging for a small memorial service to be announced in the coming week.

Mr. Ali was born on August 25, 1984, in Ravenstown, Ohio, to Abdul and Basma Ali. He graduated from Ravenstown High School in 2002.

A lover of boxing, Mr. Ali named Muhammad Ali and Diego Flores as his greatest heroes. Mr. Ali had told his friends that his goal was to pursue a law degree. He was hoping to attend community college this spring.

He is survived by his parents as well as his sister, Dimah, 14.

I put everything down and buried my face in my hands. Reading something like that had created this little pit in my stomach, a sinking feeling. I looked around my dorm room, thought about calling Aunt Sally back or even my mom, but I just thought both couldn't really change anything. It's not like I didn't believe it happened.

* * *

I got out at the end of the summer of '98, right after the Flores fight, because I had to go move in with my Aunt Sally in New Jersey. I don't think that summer was so special just because it's the last thing I took with me from Ravenstown. I know that Reggie, Tek, and Luis would probably agree that there was something about it that was different. Something mesmerizing, maybe. It's just that I know if I had tried to stay in touch with them, I'd be able to tell you whether or not that's true. But I feel that it is true, I really do. It was an important summer for all of us.

We played by the trains all the time. That's why it struck a chord with me, that it was a train accident, because they usually never mention in an obituary if they killed themself. I thought about the idea of Tek wanting to kill himself all this time, thinking about going to community college to get an advanced degree he could probably never earn while I was on a pretty college campus getting a liberal arts degree, and the self-loathing flooded in again.

The mention of his friends doing a memorial service, it's like confirmation that they're real, that they're still out there, and it made me wonder if I should be going. I thought maybe they might hate me, but I re-read the line about Diego Flores, and I know that they couldn't hate me because we did that all together during that summer. I have to believe that it matters to them as much as it matters to me. And I figure if I go back to see them, maybe we can do a better job of staying in touch.

We were just kids. We didn't know any better. We knew nothing, really. We roamed around, played with stuff, kicked things around. The woods were ours, and we made them seem like whatever we wanted them to seem like. A jungle sometimes, a castle another day. The train tracks went through the woods, and some days, it got so hot that summer there were at least three or four times one of us hallucinated about Diego Flores sitting right near us, looking at the trains with us. We fainted sometimes, but it never got too serious. We were 14 years old, and still, we daydreamed. I'd kill to have the imagination I had then. I remember the graffiti, its smooth, mesmerizing texture, the mystery of what it meant, and the way the nights just seemed to slowly turn the color of orangeade. I remember that all like it's something I still ought to be doing now. And yet, it seems so close and so foreign at the same time.

"We" was Reggie, Tek, Luis, and me: two black boys, a Hispanic boy, and myself—the black sheep white boy—all tied together by Diego Flores's poster on our walls. That, and Ravenstown. We talked about our fantasies like any boy would, but we never called it "getting out" because to do so was to acknowledge that there was a problem.

I remember the events of that summer in bits and pieces. It seems like we did the same stuff every day, like it all blended together. But that made those little changes stick out. Like these little things that happened throughout the summer actually seemed like major events; that's how routine our lives were. We were just playing by the train tracks, by the parking lots, by the alleyways, in Lou's Pizza. The summer was ours. We'd been tight for so many years, inseparable really, and we needed each other so we weren't just angry all the time because "home" was not a good place for any of us.

At the beginning, we learned about kicking stones. Diego Flores had just won that big fight over Mario Marquez. Do you remember that? Reggie said we should celebrate by throwing pebbles into the lake. We always did stuff like that when we were in a good mood, thinking about things and just relaxing. We had lots of respect for Reggie because he had the biggest Diego poster. It's kinda funny how kids pick their leader. His poster was so dark, completely black, except for the light shining down on Diego, his red trunks, his "RAVENSTOWN" tattoo that stretched from shoulder to shoulder, his arms raised triumphantly. Reggie was so dark we actually joked that the poster was the one thing blacker than him. He shrugged it off because he knew his was the best.

None of us had seen the fight, but we were talking about it. Reggie had eight siblings, so he didn't even bother trying to get his parents to let him. Tek was always in trouble with his parents, so they weren't gonna pay for it. Luis had a single mom, so he had to take care of his younger siblings all the time. I was relatively privileged, I guess, and I feel bad about that. But I also don't think they understood I had my own set of problems. I spent much of my time in front of a television, wondering when my dad would come home from his latest trucking gig. He'd always looked at me apologetically from across the living room as I was lying down with my head on my hands by the television. I'd try acting uninterested in him because I thought he was uninterested in me, and so for only a second would I turn around when I heard the opening of the screen door as he nodded his head at me without saying a word. He looked as if he wanted to say something to me most times, but he rarely did. As for my mom, she was around, but she wasn't "around." So, we never saw the fights, and I hated that I had no control over my parents.

But what we did that day, we tried to act it out ourselves. For my birthday, I had received a highlight tape of Diego, and some afternoons, we spent hour after hour watching it when we were too tired running around. Soon, we knew the highlight tape by heart, Reggie announcing one move followed by me re-enacting it on Luis, Tek offering the fake applause from the crowd. This was how we got our daily diet of Diego Flores because we were not old enough to go to the bars in town that carried the fights on television. We did it by heart that day, and every time I landed a fake Diego punch on Luis, Tek would throw a pebble into the lake, and we would count the skips. We were just kids.

This homeless guy came up to us. Old, tired-looking black guy, right up the little pebbly path by the bench where we were hanging out. We kinda just kept doing our thing because it's not like we hadn't seen homeless people before, but we were a little nervous since he seemed to be really into whatever we were doing. It was actually me who was celebrating a nice little fake punch I had landed by throwing a pretty big stone when this homeless guy just snatched it out of my hand.

"What the hell you think this is?!" the man yelled. I took a step back right away, and Reggie got right in his face, but we had to hold him back. He was screaming, and there was a little commotion and stuff, but the homeless guy just ignored us completely. He put the stone on the ground and started kicking it. We looked at him like he was crazy, like that had to hurt his feet, you know? This was a pretty decent-sized stone. The guy just didn't notice our reactions.

"Thems is kicking stones," he said defiantly as he kicked my stone past us, pointing at the other stones lying around, and then, from over his shoulder, "They ain't for throwin'. Not here."

And he kept kicking the stone along the dirt path and away from us. We looked at one another, embarrassed. Because he was older than us, it didn't matter that he was a bum. We took his word to be true because he had been wandering around longer than us, plain and simple.

Reggie found a stone and placed it on the ground. He started kicking it down the dirt path. We looked between him and the lake and followed suit, kicking stones all the way into town until we made it to Lou's Pizza, where at sunset, on this Sunday afternoon, we would get the leftover slices so long as we were first in what would become a fairly long line.

"You're a gringo," Luis told me when we sat down, "letting that old man take your stone." I blushed and looked down at my lap.

"Gringo!" Reggie and Tek yelled and laughed together, clapping their hands and belly-aching over one another, as Reggie shrieked, "Luis got jokes for Whitebread!"

This prompted Old Louie to yell at us to shut the fuck up from the back of the restaurant, us dirty, good-for-nothing brats.

"What's it mean?" Tek asked, eyeing the soda machine behind me, probably daydreaming about all its flavors.

"What's what mean?!" Reggie shouted.

"Kickin' stones, man."

"What it mean? It ain't no matter it just what you do, kick dem stones, man. What it be, what it do."

I was relieved to have lost the attention. I learned about racism, ironically, through my own experience of loneliness sometimes. Not just with my friends as the only white boy, but also that feeling of loneliness I felt when I was without them because I imagined that they felt just as alone as I did when they were the only people of color in a place. But I also learned it first-hand by watching how the three of them were treated. Immediately after that unforgivably awkward silence, Old Louie walked out, eyed the four of us, told us troublemakers to go, and to take our spic friend with us. He asked me if I was okay, and I flipped him off on my way out the door.

Dusk was setting in, and we knew we'd blown it at Lou's: we'd be hungry that night. We kicked pebbles along the crumbling plains of cement and tried to feel better. We explored the alleyways for signs of hope from others. Yes, the graffiti, our own personal horoscope, was forecasting what we knew but never said: that if a boy from Ravenstown could leave and win a boxing title, then we all could get out and be successful.

Luis shyly said he had to go to take care of his brother and sister. We all broke up for the night to make him feel better, something we had to do a lot because Luis was always busy helping his mom. He did this weird thing, though, where he would hug each of us before he left, and I think it is something his mom taught him to do. Reggie said that he was "gonna go call some chicks," the same chicks we never met, who couldn't have really existed since he spent all his time with us. Tek was absorbed by the graffiti and traced his hand along its path in the grooves of the brick wall. I think he was trying to pull the words out because they looked three-dimensional, but they ultimately frustrated him since they were not what he wanted them to be. He sauntered off without saying a word, his oversized shirt billowing in the wind against his lanky frame. Luis put his hands in his pockets and glimpsed out at the setting sun. Without looking at me, he apologized for calling me a "gringo," gave me a hug as I stood silently with my arms at my side, and trotted off to follow Tek, leaving me in the chilly evening to reflect on what didn't seem so much like a wasted day anymore, alone.

The next big thing was the day that they announced the Flores-Broxton fight. It doesn't matter where you're from, because that was a big deal. You know that Broxton was the big name in boxing at the beginning of the decade. We knew it because even as kids, we would wander into the boxing gym looking at all these guys trying to make a living, and all they would talk about was Tony Broxton. It's like you think they'd talk about Diego Flores because he was in their situation once, but no, it was all Broxton. A little Diego here and there. But when they announced the fight, all the Broxton posters were torn down off that awful, smoldering stucco in the gym. He became a public enemy, Diego a hero, and even now, as I remember the smell of sweat in that small, dingy little room on the corner of a block with empty lots, I miss the feeling of thinking that one day I was going to rise up and be just like Diego Flores.

I was watching television at home when I found out about the fight. I think I just hadn't met up with my friends yet. But I was not alone when I heard the announcement. My mom and the self-proclaimed electrician were sitting on the couch behind me. I know now that they were not really taking a moment to watch television with me. He was probably fondling her. They probably carelessly caressed one another as I sat obliviously in front of them, looking in the wrong direction, unable to understand anyway, even if I had been looking behind me. My dad had disappeared without explanation that summer, but he was always on the road so much that I hadn't even really noticed, and I was too young and stupid and preoccupied to really know what my mom was up to.

The boxing gym was where I got the news again. It was where I ran to, alone, hopping over the stones and guard rails along the sidewalks and crumbling walls, only to see fifteen to twenty men of varying ages and colors crowded around a small television on a flimsy stand in the corner of the gym. Some of them were sweaty or out of breath and had their hands at their sides. One of them was angrily wrestling with the antenna to get a better picture. Then there was Diego on the screen, cleanly shaven, with hair shorn and a crisp smile on his face that seemed so genuine. Behind the television was an autographed photograph of Diego from his younger days, when he had stepped into that very same gym. After I looked at it, I looked down at my own two feet and wondered if Diego had ever stepped in the same exact place.

I remember his smile, his white teeth, his clean-cut face, his short, spiky hair, and his general friendliness. He seemed like a guy I would hang out with, if I were older, at least. He was not just our hero, but everyone's hero. I remember wanting to lay claim to him. I remember nothing else about the interview with Diego except that they asked him where he was from, that we cheered loudly when he said "Ravenstown," and that we felt ashamed, again, when the promoter asked him, "Where the hell is that?!"

I remember the first time we actually started talking about what the fight meant. We may not have been bright kids, but we could feel things, like important moments. We were at the town dump because Reggie's mother needed a new lamp. This time, though, we weren't really looking too hard. Just talking to each other, we felt like the lamp could wait for now.

"What happens if he wins?" Tek asked, plunging his long arms into a dirty pile of empty beer cans.

"Why you always be askin' stupid questions, man?" Reggie yelled. Just Reggie being Reggie, I thought. Tek shrugged.

"Dunno, man. Just curious ..."

At first, I had agreed with Reggie that Tek was asking a dumb question. But they weren't always dumb. I mean, even the question about kicking stones seemed dumb at first, but then you really had to think about it. Yeah, if Diego Flores won, he'd be the champion. He'd be the best. But then what? What did it really mean? What happened next?

Luis, already tan in his white tank top, put the matter to rest. He was good at doing that ever so quietly while I, I just kept kicking and digging through piles like I normally would.

"If he wins, he's the welterweight champion, Tek. Best in the world. As for what happens after that, man, I dunno. We gonna find out, though, right?"

Eventually, the conversation turned to what it might mean

for us. We all had our own dreams, but we hardly talked about them openly.

"So ... what you gon' do?" Tek asked.

Reggie shrugged, a look of frustration marking his sweaty face. "Dunno, man. Boxing, probably. How 'boutchu?"

Tek raised his shoulders as well, then bent over to pick up a stone. He studied it a bit, turning it over in his hands, tossing it from one to the other. He turned around to throw it into the lake, extending his arm backward, but then he stopped, put it on the ground, and tapped it with his foot.

"I dunno."

Was he too ashamed to tell us he wanted to be a lawyer?

* * *

We walked home. But walking home those days wasn't just plain and simple like it should've been. We'd jump on rails and hop between the blocks of cement or jump into the holes that had formed within the blocks. We pretended to be other people: the President of the United States, a famous actor, Diego Flores. We thought we were free, and maybe we were. No one was around to tell us otherwise during those walks in the darkness. And no one cared that summer about where we were or what time we'd be home for dinner.

That was the problem. Sometimes, I'd get home, and my mother would be absent. If I was lucky, I'd get a note next to some food. It would say that she was out for the night but here was some food for dinner. Other times, no note and no food. There were many nights when I didn't eat a real dinner. I was used to scrounging around, and I don't know if my mother knew that and budgeted accordingly, but I managed.

Other times, she would be home. If she was with a man, she would instantly explain his purpose. He would be an electrician, or a plumber, or a mechanic, or something that we apparently needed over for some kind of fixing. They would always wave to me awkwardly and try to be my friend. I was too naïve to think that they were there for any other purpose. Usually, these men would leave pretty quickly after I had arrived.

Whether or not someone was over, she would ask me what I was up to. She'd ask if I was "kicking around town." Usually, that was the right way of putting it. A few times, when she asked me this kind of question, she seemed to mean it. Sometimes she seemed to feel genuinely sorry about being a shitty mom. She would swing back her black hair and narrow her eyes at me, making me feel like she was really listening. Without fail, I'd brush her off as quickly as possible and go to watch television. And I don't see how I can regret that.

I got home one day from sitting by the train tracks (we had been watching the trains come and go through town all day), and my mother stood up and instantly came to the door to give me a hug. She was wearing only jeans and a bra.

She peppered me with kisses and hugs and asked me how I was feeling. I was confused by her sudden affection, but I tried to enjoy it. It was a surprisingly good feeling to think that she might love me. She asked me if I was looking forward to school, what I had been doing with my friends, what I thought about Diego's upcoming fight. She even led me to the kitchen table and sat me down on the chair next to hers, got up on her knees on the chair, and started blowing smoke rings. She asked me if I wanted to go watch the Diego Flores fight somewhere in a month.

I actually started to look at her for once. Of course, I'd seen her around, but I didn't really know what she looked like up close. She had beautiful green eyes, long dark hair, and a bony frame. Her narrow jawline and wrinkles made her look kind of like a witch, but a beautiful witch, I thought to myself. Yes, maybe I loved my mother after all.

"So, um … where's Dad?" I finally asked. I thought that this was my chance. All summer, I had been curious, but my mother and I barely spoke. I thought that even the slightest hint of this question would get me into some kind of trouble. Either that, or I was afraid to know the answer. To me, it was possible that my dad had died. I had noticed him fighting with my mom, so I thought to myself that maybe she wouldn't have even been sad if he had died. Maybe she even killed him. I really wouldn't have known either way.

She put out her cigarette and looked at me in a cold way. She had never looked at me like that before. I can still see that look in my head when I want to conjure it. It was a sympathetic stare, right into my eyes. But I realize now it was just a look of insecurity.

"Do you love me?" she asked. I shook. Love was not a word that was used in that house. I hadn't remembered my parents saying anything about love except for when I was younger, when they tucked me in at night. I remembered it then only because I didn't remember it ever happening afterward. What I knew then was teddy bears from my mother, catch with my father, and that I was loved. With time, that all gradually dissolved. The hardest part about leaving them behind was that I like to think that my mom and dad are still those people, that they're in there somewhere, but I can't have them.

I looked down and clamped my hands together. I didn't really know what love was. Even if I had loved my mother, I was shy about admitting it, just as I was shy about letting Luis hug me before he went home every night. But I knew there was only one way to get what I wanted out of this conversation, and besides, my mom had just showered me with affection for the first time since God knows when. I had thought that maybe I did love her, or at least admire her in some weird way, because she seemed beautiful.

"Yes," I muttered.

"Oh, that makes me so happy to hear," she said, sliding the traces of cocaine off the table. It's a detail that I hadn't really noticed back then.

"You know, sometimes I feel bad I'm not around and everything. Your Aunt Sally has all the money in the world, and she still doesn't help her sister out. But I always know you're doing just fine. You and those kids. Oh, boys will be boys," she chuckled, but then, seeing me sitting there emotionless, added, "Yes ... you boys are something else."

I nodded.

"Dad's gone away for a while, a lot of long drives out west somewhere. But he'll be back sometime."

She gave me a hug. And that was that.

*   *   *

As July turned into August, the heat grew worse, but the town was buzzing with the upcoming fight. Ravenstown was getting press. People were becoming friendlier. We still sat by the train tracks and watched the trains come and go. We wondered if we could hop on board. Reggie dared us to try, but none of us were brave enough. I still wonder if Tek was giving it a try.

We played games. We searched for things. We jumped and hopped around. But mostly, we sat down against the tree trunks by the tracks and fiddled with leaves, getting ready for the next train to come. We didn't carry watches with us, but it was so routine for us, and we could tell time so well just with our senses that we knew when each train would come. We just wondered where it would come from, where it would go to. We could never prove who was right or wrong, and because we were never wrong, the game was always fun.

A week before the fight, we thought we had another one of those weird hallucinations, except the sun was setting, and we were getting ready to go home. About fifty yards down the tracks from us was a shirtless man panting heavily on a tree stump looking out at the tracks. He was real sweaty. We hadn't seen him. Reggie was the one who elbowed us and silently motioned toward him. And after a really long, hard stare, we all had the sneaking suspicion that this person was none other than Diego Flores himself.

We inched closer, following Reggie's lead.

"Oh my God," Luis said. We were only twenty-five yards or so away now, and the man had turned to face us. It really was Diego.

We stopped. We looked at him. He looked at us. His face was wet with sweat, and he was breathing heavily. He had probably been running through the woods. He was cut like a rock. He was hunched over just enough so that we could see the edges of his "Ravenstown" tattoo. It really was him.

My first thought was, "What is he doing here?" I had imagined Diego Flores as a celebrity who had left Ravenstown for good. He was the kind of person who would live in Los Angeles. Or just anywhere else, really. Places that were far away.

We all had that thought as we sat there with stupid expressions on our faces. Finally, Diego motioned for us to come over. We jogged over immediately, and for the first and last time in our lives, we saw the legend up close. He was a real person, after all. He extended his hand and said, "Diego." We shook it one by one, mumbling our names, never once looking anywhere else but at his face.

"What are you boys doing here?" he asked. His voice confirmed that this was really him, not a robot that just looked like him or something. We had only seen and heard him on television.

"We just lookin' at dem trains," Reggie replied. "How 'boutchu?"

"I used to do that all the time," Diego said, looking out at the tracks and ignoring Reggie's question altogether. "I figured I'd revisit my roots, do a little bit of training, some shadow-boxing like I used to do. Get some perspective."

"What's perspective?" I asked quietly.

There was a long silence. Then I noticed. He had wet eyes. Not from sweating, but from crying. He really was human after all, I thought. My hero had weaknesses just like anyone else. He really was a person, wasn't he?

"Why you cryin'?" Reggie asked. I think the rest of us

wanted to hit him. He was being so bold, trying to impress Diego. But the boxer just laughed.

"I saw you kids; made me remember what it was like to be a kid here."

"You didn't like being a kid here?"

"I loved being a kid here, man. When all of your life is still ahead of you and you are full of hope; someday you will look back on it and think about it and miss it."

It felt weird that Diego admired us as much as we admired him, and we didn't really understand what he was saying, nor had he answered my question about perspective, so we all felt coy and kept quiet. He broke the silence.

"You kids remind me of me and my boys."

"Where are your boys?" Diego sighed.

"They're part of my posse. They live by me in Queens. It's in New York. But the other dude I was tight with, me and my buddy dared him to jump onto one of those trains and get outta here, and he did it."

"So, he's somewhere else now?"

"No," Diego said. "It was an accident."

Now, everyone was quiet.

"Do a lot of boxers cry?" Luis asked, taking Reggie's lead.

"They all cry."

"Dag," Reggie said, "That's wild, son."

I imagined Tony Broxton crying. I couldn't see it. It was acceptable for my hero, Diego, because he was a real man. But for that brute Tony Broxton, there was no crying allowed.

"You gonna win that fight, yo?" Tek chimed in, gesticulating nervously with his hands.

Diego laughed again.

"Sure hope so, buddy."

It was my turn to talk. I asked him what had been on my mind all summer.

"You think we'll get out, too?"

Diego looked at me anxiously with his mouth closed and

seemed to be really studying me. It made me nervous. Then he sighed and looked down at the ground and then back out at the tracks with his head on his fist, shaking his head, not saying a single word.

When I got home that night, I was excited to tell my mom about what had just happened. Not only had I met my hero, but I also found out that only one of the four of myself and my friends needed to make it in order for us to get out and make something of ourselves. There was nothing else in the world besides Diego Flores that would make me so anxious to see her. But when I opened the door, she wasn't there. I saw my Aunt Sally, my Uncle Gary, and some other guy I had never seen before sitting at the kitchen table, waiting for me. I hadn't seen my aunt and uncle in years, but I recognized them all the same. I liked them even though I rarely saw them because they always sent me money for my birthday. My mom always took most of it, but I was conditioned to think they were good people. Still, my first instinct was to run. They opened their mouths to say something, so I ran.

I ran as fast as I could down the street. I knew if I could just get to the woods, then I would have a major advantage. I realized pretty quickly that the stranger, the stranger who had stood up when I opened the door, was chasing after me. He forced me toward the lake, and when I got there, I could only give up.

He calmed me down on the way back to the house, and he told me I was going to have to live with my aunt and uncle for a while. Apparently, my mother was in jail. I know now that he was some kind of child protection agent or something. I know now that he found me a way out without even meaning to. The whole thing wasn't a big deal to me at the time because the Diego Flores fight was coming up, and I had just met the man himself, and having different parents wasn't going to change much, I thought.

When we got back to the house, Uncle Gary and Aunt Sally gave me a hug and told me everything would be alright. I ignored them and asked where they lived. All I really knew was that they were from somewhere else. When they said New Jersey, I tried to run again, but the strange man held me back. I kicked and screamed; I have never been more upset in my life. In the years that followed, I slowly began to see it as a blessing, but I'm never completely sure it was because it makes me feel so strange, thinking about all these things that could have been. The parents I had who disappeared. The friends I had who I betrayed.

I kicked and screamed so much that they begged me to tell them what was the matter. When I told them about the Flores fight, they looked at each other and shrugged and told me we could stay around for a week before we left, in a motel or something. I know they were trying to do anything they could to help me.

The next week was the hardest one of my life. I lived in a motel in the next town over with Uncle Gary and Aunt Sally. They tried to offer me all kinds of different things, but I refused. All I wanted to do was hang out with Reggie, Tek, and Luis. To Uncle Gary and Aunt Sally, it was absurd that I was allowed to wander around all day without any parental supervision, and they thought I might run away again if they let me do what I was used to doing.

There were a few times I was able to invite them all over to go swimming in the motel pool. The first time they came, I denied that anything was happening. I told them that my aunt and uncle were visiting from out of town and that I was just staying with them for the week. I don't know why I lied to them. I think I was too young to feel guilty because even though we felt like we needed to get out of Ravenstown, we still had dreams and everything. I think it was because I was scared, or I didn't want to actually believe it myself that I was going to be leaving them behind.

The one day Aunt Sally and Uncle Gary did let me go off on my own, though, was the day Diego had his fight. The day that happened, there was a parade in town. Lou's was giving out free pizza, everyone was smiling, and people were drinking in the streets; it was really a sight to see in Ravenstown.

The euphoria came to a bit of a standstill at seven o'clock when most of these people tried to crowd into bars to watch the fight itself. The bars were really the only places in town that could carry the fight. Fortunately, Reggie, Tek, Luis, and I had every intention of watching it together. I just didn't know if I really felt like I was one of them anymore. I could tell they knew there was something wrong, but we just got used to never asking each other what kinds of personal problems we had.

We went to the Purple Raven, which was the most popular bar in town and probably the most crowded that night. The bouncer, this odd-looking bald guy with thick eyelashes and thin lips, glared at us as we came to the door. He signaled his counterpart over from inside the bar, a taller black man with sunglasses and dreadlocks who looked upset about having to focus his attention away from the thumping music within the bar.

The white guy whispered something to the black guy, and the black guy just simply said, "No," and shooed us away with his hands.

"C'mon, man, please?" Reggie begged. "We been waitin' all summer for this. C'mon, man."

"You kids ain't twenty-one," the bouncer said. We looked at each other, then at the bouncer. There was a long line behind us. Soon, they took our side.

"Let the kids in," they shouted, or, "Do it for Ravenstown!"

The bouncer blushed, and his fat friend started whispering in his ear again. The other bouncer started nodding his head.

"Alright, fine. You kids can come in. But you gotta pay the five-dollar cover."

Between the four of us, we could manage the $2.71 that we had in our pockets, just loose change we had collected on the sidewalks or in the woods. The people behind us took note of the situation and started collecting money amongst themselves. Soon, they had collected $18 and had forked it over to the bouncer. He made this fake smile and let us in, shoving the wad of cash into his pocket.

The bar was dingy, dark, and reeking of piss and booze. We didn't care. The music was loud, the television was showing the fights that led up to the title bout, and we were really just amazed with our first experience: hundreds of happy people crammed into one space. Had they always been that happy? Had we just never known?

People said things to us here and there about how young we were, but soon, we were seeing several other people arrive at the bar who were clearly under 21 as well. We were left alone toward the back of the bar to watch the moment we had been waiting all summer for, if not our whole lives.

There was a buzz when we saw Tony Broxton on the screen. The bar, mostly crowded with men, felt electric. The men were of all different shapes, sizes, and colors. Many of them wore hats, clinked their glasses together, and gazed upwards at the televisions in anticipation. In the past, these men had fought each other in this bar. Today, they were friends.

I looked at my own friends, but they were all captivated by the television. For me, it was less of a marvel because television was my daily life when I was not with them. I also knew I was leaving, and my mind was elsewhere. My friends, they were silent but anxious. Tek was biting his fingernails.

Then, Diego Flores came on the screen. There was a loud roar as he walked to the ring and took off his warm-ups. In the past, Diego had seemed like a distant figure to us. But now, he seemed quite real. It was only a week ago that we had spoken to him right after one of his workouts by the train tracks during a little foray into his roots before the big fight.

I noticed two things before the fight started. First, I noticed that Tony Broxton was enormous. He looked invincible. Seeing him was the reminder that what we had expected to happen all along was far from given. The euphoria we had experienced earlier that day was there because we needed it. We couldn't risk waiting until after the fight because Diego might lose.

The second thing I noticed was that this did not deter anyone from being hopeful. Yes, the others around me had noticed it, too, that Broxton was a bull. They fidgeted nervously. They were sweating; the bar stank like sweat. They chatted nervously with one another. Nothing was certain for any of us. But they were still smiling.

When the fight started, the bar became more silent as people focused on the match. When there was a flurry of activity, there were excited roars. Occasionally, people called things out to the television. But if Tony Broxton ever did anything good, the place was dead silent, and we just watched and waited and hoped.

For the first couple of rounds, there was little action. Broxton was slightly more active than Flores. Me and my friends knew very little about boxing, but we knew enough to tell who was winning; plus, we could tell by the noises people made in the bar. Throughout the first two rounds, we had been muttering instructions to Flores. He needs to duck quicker. He needs to land some more jabs. He's gotta hop-step. Or, from Reggie, he gotta fuckin' pick it up.

As the fight continued, Flores started to develop his chances. By the sixth round, he had Broxton cornered and landed a huge uppercut on the jaw before time ran out. The bar erupted. The tides were turning. Our hometown hero was taking control of the bout. As he walked back to his corner with a bloody eye, I thought about the tears that had emanated from that eye only a week ago. I thought about how blessed I was to have met this man. I thought about how he was the brother I had always wanted. And then I looked at my friends and thought to myself that these were the brothers I wanted for the rest of my life. In that moment, I realized that I loved each of them dearly in their own special way. I wanted to tell them that I loved them, but it seemed out of place not only for that time but for any time we were hanging out together. After all, we were four boys from the Midwest, and we couldn't have known much about feelings. We threw pebbles. We kicked stones. We ran around. We played with things. We looked at the trains. We looked to Diego. We smelled the beer and the blood, but we didn't know the fighting first-hand. We knew we were supposed to feel hopeless, but somehow, we had this enthusiasm to stir around. We couldn't have known a thing at all. I thought about just telling them that I was leaving, but the fight was about to continue.

When the seventh round picked up, Diego continued where he had left off. But Broxton would not go down. He was very much in the fight, landing his jabs here and there. And then, as quickly as I had regained hope on a hot summer day in front of my television, I instantly lost it all as Tony Broxton landed a shattering blow across Diego's right cheek, knocking him unconscious down to the ground like a lightning bolt.

Except for the people that cried out in despair, the bar was utterly silent. I felt a weight enter my stomach. I looked at my friends, their mouths agape at the television. I looked back at the television to confirm my worst fears: Diego, lying motionless on the ground, as Tony Broxton raised his arms in victory and hugged his trainer, sweat and blood dripping down from his crew cut down to his legs.

We hung our heads. I felt bad. For myself, yes, but more so for my friends. Would it be strange if I said I missed that feeling of despair we had? Usually, this was the time when fights would start. Yes, men were starting to yell expletives out in the air. These men had been coming here to sweat out their anger for years. They had fought each other. They knew one another quite well. They worked with one another. They kept each other down in their daily lives. The time was ripe for a beating, or several. We were young, but we knew that, so we inched toward the door.

But all I remember as I was leaving was the men crying. My friends didn't see it; they were so eager to leave. It was just me looking back from the doorway before one of them grabbed my arm and pulled me out. I wish they could have seen it. Grown men crying, just like Diego. Grown men crying and hugging and comforting each other. I have this image in my head of a man with short hair and a little bit of a beard sobbing into his arms over a beer and two Hispanic strangers holding themselves close to him. My friends were angry, and they expected the mood to reflect their own feelings of sadness. But they couldn't have known what the atmosphere would be like, the throes of compassion in a time of utter solitude, so we got out of that place, kicking stones the whole way home.

A BOY'S SCHOOL —

We knew that day, that first day of senior year, that things were about to be different and that our lives were going to change. We anticipated the great stories we would tell about events that hadn't happened yet. We knew that we would become closer, we would win some games and lose some, we would have sex with girls, we would meet college counselors, we would know all of each other's grades, and we would all compete to get into different schools and then eventually part ways. Well, we knew that ten of the fifty of us would probably go on to Harvard together or something like that and that the rest of us might be lucky to have a fellow Ashbury Latin alum at their new college. We knew all that. But what we all eventually learned is that there was a lot we didn't know.

Five years ago, when we were sixies, we didn't know much at all. There were only 40 of us then. We looked at all the older boys in wide-eyed wonder; we were curious about the stories we overheard in the student lounge about their sexual exploits, and we were terrified whenever they reminded us of the difficulties that lay ahead of us in the area's foremost and one of the country's top recognized boys' day schools. Our soon-to-be home defied elitist expectations by having the lowest tuition amongst its peers, bringing in the area's brightest and most racially and financially diverse population. While some of us belonged in a Nantucket clothing catalog, the rest of us paid only a fraction of the pricey tuition and took the city bus to and from school every day, struggling to pay the $50 yearly class dues. But while it seemed progressive on that front, almost everything else about our experience was austere, from the school's draconian policies around off-campus alcohol consumption to the tattered sports uniforms we wore in competition against peers from other local schools. Merely forgetting to make eye contact with a teacher and to greet them by name in the hallway could get you into some sort of trouble.

We were 40 boys before eighth grade, when we added Joey Mazilli to the fold. He had a slick way of talking, and we were all surprised by the way he wasn't scared of any of us, even though we were all best friends, and he was a stranger. And then, freshman year, we added another 11, a group that usually fills holes in the class: a great singer (Teddy McShay); a big, bad football player (Big Frank Brown); and an all-around good student from a low-income family (Leon Williams), to name a few. This was after Eric Tompkins left (couldn't handle it, and none of us liked him much anyway) and Steven Shettel moved to California with his family (he eventually got into Stanford). So, then we were 50.

Sophomore year was when some of us started having sex. Slowly, we found that the locker room gossip we used to overhear was now being brought about more and more by some of us. We were starting to listen less and talk more. It had started freshman year when Big Head Ted bragged about his first blowjob for weeks. Except he didn't admit it was his first. Either way, I remember being quite embarrassed and feeling a little awkward about myself because I hadn't done much with girls yet. I always felt insecure listening to other people brag about it, and I didn't want to ask questions. As it turned out, Big Head Ted told us that he was really deserving of his nickname now that he was getting head on a regular basis. It didn't seem to bother him that his arrogance kind of bothered us.

But there were other rumblings beginning sophomore year. Sometimes, you could hear it in the student lounge. We were dating now. Mostly girls from our sister school, Orchard Valley, which was only a few minutes away in the city. But there were other all-girl schools with lesser reputations, and with those lesser reputations came lower standards, and for the most part, it was those girls with whom some of us were starting to fool around.

With the introduction of sex, drugs and alcohol slowly followed, but they only really made their presence felt in junior year and among only a few of us. The school had a strict drug and alcohol policy. If they ever found out you had so much as a sip of alcohol—even outside of school—you could get expelled. So I was also a late bloomer in that regard, though me and my best friend, Denny Salley, started to drink a little bit, just the two of us, at the end of junior year, always making sure that we'd keep it between just us, even in times when we might have gained some street cred by telling others. We had never really drank before, so we had our fair share of incidents.

Junior year, I also had my first real girlfriend. I had others before here and there, but it's really hard to say that those counted. I hadn't known much. I classify this "real" girlfriend as real because it actually lasted more than a few months. She went to one of those less reputable girls' schools, but within that community, I'd have to say (though I was kind of biased) that she was probably an exception to the rule. She was a real sweetheart, and not only did she bolster my reputation among my girl-crazy classmates, but she also broke my heart because she was a year older and chose the adventures of college over the same old dinner and movie dates with me. Couple that with the death of my grandfather a month before we broke up, and I was having bouts of depression through the end of my junior spring and on into the following year. In retrospect, much of it was just teenage angst. But there was truth in my sadness: I was starting to realize that people would let me down in life and that nothing good would last forever. My parents had picked up on something going on, so they sent me to see a therapist whose job it was to remind me that I still had some kind of worth when he wasn't falling asleep listening to my rants.

I think this story starts in my mind when Jimmy Chambers

finally let the cat out of the bag about his SAT scores. He was one of those guys who was pretty good at a lot of things—not amazing, but still enough to be considered an all-around performer at AL. Jimmy was really tight with another guy in our class, Allen Berkowitz, and a lot of us would tease them from time to time that they were gay. But I think what it comes down to is that maybe some of us were jealous of their success; after all, they had won two of the four book awards the spring before, and their other good friend, Alex Mint, had won the third. I never had any problems with Jimmy. No one did, really. We all hassled each other because that is what you do when you are a teenager trying to fit in.

Anyway, we were sitting in a school-wide assembly we call "hall" in the morning before class. It was one of those long, boring halls where we had some Jewish guy coming in to talk to us about the upcoming major holidays. Our wooden chairs were squeaking as the restless amongst us constantly shifted positions. Big Frank Brown was sitting to my right, and he kept elbowing me in the ribs as a joke because I kept falling asleep. Everyone was so tired all the time; school was so tough.

When the thing was finally over, and Headmaster Browning called "Class One," we rose, and immediately, I heard Joey Mazilli—who had been sitting to my left—talking to Jimmy in what was apparently a conversation that had started before the hall.

"So, we're between 1400 and 1500 ... that's pretty broad, man. I mean, that's the difference between Swarthmore and Harvard. Nothing against Swarthmore, you don't seem like a Swarthmore guy, you're too cool for that school, for those nerd-burglars ..."

Jimmy looked frustrated. His face was reddening, and he had clearly noticed the other ears around him that had perked up.

"I'd say it's closer to 'Harvard' then, but that's really it ..."

I wondered if maybe Jimmy was thinking Harvard. He didn't seem like a Harvard guy. Not that he didn't have the credentials, but everyone knew Joey was hell-bent on capitalizing on the AL name and going down that path, and if there was any reason Jimmy wouldn't want to talk to Joey about it, maybe it was part of that competitive nature we always saw from him on the soccer field and the wrestling mat.

That's when Allen intervened and gave Joey a light shove. He had actually bumped into me because he was right behind me and could overhear the conversation. "Buddy, let him be."

Allen was a pretty built guy. He was captain of the wrestling team and, like I said, very well respected. Joey, with his greasy, slicked-back hair and beady eyes, was exactly the opposite. It was like watching a lion paw at a mouse.

"1550?" Joey craned his neck around Allen, who had placed his two hands firmly on Joey's chest. Jimmy blushed and then shrugged his arching shoulders apprehensively. With a crooked smile, he replied, "You got it, man. What can I say?"

And that's how we figured out Jimmy's SAT score. Joey called him a rat bastard and gave him a pat on the back, and for the rest of the day, that's what we talked about. Jimmy was really one of the last ones to tell us, or at least the last guy who had a legitimate shot to go Ivy.

It probably continued in the lounge. At least, that's where I first picked up on it, during third period after senior English was out. There was a congregation of guys—I distinctly remember Tony Flanders leading the charge (Mazilli had class)—who were just ranting about Jimmy's SAT score. Admittedly, a pang of jealousy had swept over me when I heard it first-hand. But there was no time to dwell on such insecurities; the moment I walked through the door, Big Head Ted called from across the room.

"Yo! Richie! You were there for that shit, right? 1550? Are you serious?"

I nodded my head and, in the process of doing so, implicated myself in this guilty scheme of jealous scuttlebutting that had plagued most of us for the past five years.

I say that this story started then because it's the best and earliest memory I have of Jimmy being under stress that year.

But the story could begin anywhere. It could begin with sixie year because he was the first boy in the class I'd met. I fondly remember feeling slighted that I was the second boy he'd met—Theo Smith was the first, and the first black person Jimmy had ever met in his life, which is hard for me to forget—but I'd soon get over that. Or there was another time in eighth grade when I had brought my lunch to school and dropped my sandwich on the floor. I must have looked like I was about to cry because Jimmy immediately offered me half of his.

But it began then because I had forced him out of the periphery of my memory, and I recall that as the last time I'd be able to do that in my life with anything. As I look back on it now, I tell myself that the story had to begin then because I was so traumatized by what happened and unable to push it out of my mind that I had to think about the last time I could push something out of my mind in order to try to cure myself. And even if it was the random time we gossiped about Jimmy's SAT score, it had to be something.

It had been a typical day. Homeroom went by. Salim Singh (our class president) read the announcements, and we, for the most part, listened to half of it. We were just too tired. We, of course, hissed when he spoke about planning the upcoming social with Terhune, and we cheered when he reported the Varsity Soccer team's 5–0 exhibition thrashing of Fillerton on the Hill. That's where Jimmy comes in: I distinctly remember not seeing him in that madness, our proud captain of the soccer team. Something struck me as that moment being particularly strange and inappropriate, and though I did not feel the emptiness then, it's an emptiness that I feel about that moment when thinking back all the time.

Latin class went on as usual during the first period. Mr. Branagan, an esteemed teacher of over thirty years at the school, read off our quiz scores publicly. This form of public humiliation had motivated me to succeed in Latin when I was a fifthie in Mr. Branagan's class. At AL, it was not okay to be a lot of

things: a virgin, a homo, a loser, whatever—but if there was anything you didn't want to be, it was dumb. And it was during that
moment of timid anticipation that Salim Singh burst into the
class and told us that we had to leave immediately because there
was an emergency hall. I felt an emptiness inside my stomach.
The last time something like this had happened was a few years
ago when two planes had crashed into the World Trade Center.
We looked at each other in wide-eyed silence, muttered a word
or two, and then rushed out of the room.

Other students were congregating and flooding through the
creaky hallways and down the wooden stairs toward Ashenfelter
Hall. We whispered anxiously to each other about the possible
explanations for this disturbance. Was there another terrorist
attack? God, that would be awful. Maybe it was some new kind
of catastrophe. What came with the fear for me was also a slight
sense of excitement about the unknown, and I have felt guilty
for having that feeling for a long time now.

One of these images that I've preserved in my memory
forever is the expression on Headmaster Browning's face as
we locked eyes when I entered the Hall. He was supremely
grim-looking, and he had these paunchy cheeks and laser-like
lines running under his eyes as if he had not slept in days. He
had been talking closely with Assistant Headmaster Cork, and
I soon realized that Headmaster Browning's clerical collar (he
was also a priest at a local Church and often reminded us of the
old maxim "From those to whom much has been given, much
will be expected") was ruffled and twisted. I noticed because
Assistant Headmaster Cork fixed it for him in that split-sec-
ond of time that my eyes met with Headmaster Browning's,
and I realized that the man who knew all—the man who had
been told about the great disaster—was even more fearful than
I was because he had to deliver terrible news.

I solemnly took my seat toward the front with the other
seniors and folded my hands over my lap. My heart was beating very quickly, and even though everyone else was looking

at one another for an explanation, I tried to act respectably. It appeared that we were relatively late arrivals, aside from a few sixies who were appearing here and there, not really understanding one way or the other why we held these halls 65 times a year in the first place. Ultimately, I couldn't help but rubberneck; as I craned my head around the blob that was Big Frank Brown behind me, I could see Headmaster Browning conferring with Mrs. Sheridan, the sixie group leader. Shortly thereafter, they parted ways, and Headmaster Browning adjusted his jacket, kept his head down, and walked with determination to the front of the room.

The clapping of his black dress shoes against the rusty, wood-paneled floor was the only noise that reverberated in the hall. It seemed like a painfully long time that he walked, and you could tell he felt all the eyes that were on him because he was constantly arranging and then rearranging his hands around his jacket. We remember the way he hesitated at the steps as if he reconsidered telling us. But then, after that first step, he popped up the other two as if making up for lost time. We talked about that later on. We wondered what was going through his head. When he got to the top of the stairs, he looked out at us, sighed, fixed his jacket again, and squared his attention on the podium. When he got to the podium, he deliberately placed his hands on either side and squeezed and looked straight into its wooden surface before taking a deep breath and raising his head.

"Boys, this is no easy task, I assure you that ..."

As his voice trailed off, I noticed myself more dialed in than any other previous hall I had attended in all my years at the school.

"It is with great, great sorrow and sadness that I must inform you that senior Jimmy Chambers was in a serious car accident last night. As he was driving home after the varsity soccer exhibition game, he fell asleep at the wheel, crossed the median line, and crashed into a tree on the opposite side of the road. He is currently comatose, and we received word of all this just now, and that it is unclear if he will survive."

From the back of the room, we could hear Mr. Gittlin shriek "No!" among the others. Mr. Gittlin was Jimmy's advisor for all six years. The last sentence had sent the hall into an uproar, and Headmaster Browning backed away from the podium to let the news sink in. He had tears in his eyes. It was one of those situations where you know the bad news, but you're waiting to find out just how bad it is. As I've learned now, whenever you hear about someone who dies, you never know the extent of the bad news until that fateful last line. It's always, "He fell," or "He had an accident," or "He wasn't looking," and then, almost every time, "He died."

As for me, the world lost its shape and structure all at once. Everything was moving so fast in front of my eyes, and yet nothing was happening at all. It was a dizzying madness of misperception, as if I was being shaken so much that I could not use my senses. And yet, I could still see that we were all just sitting at the same time. And yet, in the back of my mind, this negative voice that had begun plaguing me for the last several months made itself heard again. "Of course this happened," it said to me. "Bad things will always happen all around you."

Headmaster Browning regained his poise.

"After conferring with Assistant Headmaster Cork, we've decided it would be best to cancel class today. When more details are made available to us, we will share them with you. At the current time, it would be best for everyone to pray for Jimmy today and return tomorrow and attempt to move forward the best that we can. Counseling will be made available to any student; please speak with Dean Charles if you have any questions about that. I'll only ask that members of Class One please meet in the Lecture Hall immediately after the hall before dismissing themselves."

He seemed to have mastered the situation by now, but he was still concerned. You could see it in the way he delicately paused over each word as he simultaneously took in our reactions. For him, the grieving process had to occur quickly. He was more worried about us, his children, and he would not allow himself to look weak. He was probably ashamed for shedding a tear.

"God bless you all, boys, and be strong. My last feeling is that, well, is that you stand up and that we observe a moment of silence before saying a prayer."

We stood up on command, like zombies. I placed my hands on the chiseled wooden chair in front of me. Someone had carved their initials, and to the right of that, the school's Latin motto: *mortui vivos docent* (the dead teach the living).

It was an impregnable silence, and still, I remember how it seemed to resonate within me like the plucked string of some delicate instrument, shaking my foundations without really moving me at all. I did the logical thing: I thought of Jimmy. It all seemed surreal. Just last week, we found out about his SAT score, and he was humble and disappointed all at once, and now he was gone for no apparent reason at all. I didn't cry, but I did feel sorry, and I wondered what the odds were that Jimmy might live. Then, without warning, the Lord's Prayer:

Pater noster, qui es in caelis,
sanctificetur nomen tuum. Adveniat regnum tuum.
Fiat voluntas tua, sicut in caelo et in terra. Panem nostrum quo-
tidianum da nobis hodie, et dimitte nobis debita nostra
sicut et nos dimittimus debitoribus nostris. Et ne nos inducas in
tentationem,
sed libera nos a malo. Amen.

"Class One," Headmaster Browning said, raising his index finger. We departed unceremoniously and in unison, unsure of whether or not to console each other. Not yet. Too soon.

As I meandered to the back of the hall, I saw Mr. Gittlin sobbing. I was oblivious to the possibility that teachers could be on the same level as us, full of emotion, confusion, equals on a level playing field. He had, as it appeared, just found out, just like the rest of us. What's more is that he had a more palpable reaction than any of my classmates, except perhaps Allen, whom I hadn't spotted yet. It's not to say that no one cared because quite the opposite was true: several of my peers were sobbing, and as it became clear over time, they were very upset about the news. But there was something altogether startling about the discovery that our teachers cared about us more than just as students. We always knew we had special relationships with the faculty that probably would not occur in a different kind of school. I just never thought they would cry over us.

That reality became even more apparent as I stepped outside to take the shortcut to the lecture hall. Some of my classmates were with me, and others went the longer way indoors. Regardless, I had not yet mustered the courage to speak to any of them.

There was no time, as it turned out. Mr. Stevens, my advisor for the past three years, grabbed me by the arm. I hadn't seen him. It's like he was lurking outside the whole time, waiting for me.

He led me a few steps away from the front of the school by the senior grass, far enough away from everyone else that we could speak privately. Mr. Stevens was my favorite teacher, and he had been for the past few years, which is why I chose him as my advisor. He was like a close friend, and part of that was because he was so young and good-looking that I felt popular and attractive myself just by being in his presence so frequently. Things that were not my business—his girlfriends, his weekends, his college stories—became my unexpected gift every week that we met over a period of time as he gradually became more comfortable with me. I reciprocated by telling him every living fear in my soul.

"Richie," he said, and then, grabbing me by the shoulders and shaking me, "Richie. Richie!"

I looked up at him, squinting against the sunlight, still in a fatigued haze and overwhelmed by its force.

"Richie, I just want you to know that you will get through this. If you need to talk about anything, *anything*"—he pointed his finger as he emphasized it—"then I will be here for you. Do you understand?"

I nodded my head slowly, and he started up again.

"I know you were depressed about Maria last year, and I know how down you can get. I'm worried about you."

"I'll be okay," I said, motioning toward my classmates who had almost completely filed out of the double wooden doors in front of the school. He bit his lip, but he understood. I thanked him, immediately regretted that my shock over his repeated inquiries led to such dismissiveness, and trudged away in silence.

The lecture hall was, as I recollect, a terrifying scene. In a lighter way, it reminded me of being in the locker room sophomore year when our football team was losing 30–0 to Oceanside Academy at halftime. No one spoke. People had tears in their eyes as they stared into the nothingness ahead of them in disbelief, appearing transplanted from some other ghastly world beyond the one we were in. Some of us shook our heads, crossed our arms, and swore silently. We all had different ways of dealing with it. Then there was Allen.

Allen had, apparently, cursed at some sad-looking sixie, telling him that he didn't even know Jimmy, so why the fuck was he sad? Allen was the most vocal among us, muttering things out loud and mourning without any kind of outward self-consciousness. Some of us didn't know what to do. We wanted to apologize to him, but we were perplexed by our own feelings for a couple of reasons. First, Jimmy hadn't died—there was no real "loss" to apologize for. And secondly, it was a shared misfortune. Who do you say "sorry" to when it affects everyone else the same? I guess it just seemed right that we apologize to him because he was the closest to Jimmy, and even though it was all of our loss that he was in such bad shape, it was Allen's before ours. So, some of us, myself included, went up to Allen, and we just gave him a hug. Under any other circumstances, it would have been weird and we would call each other homos. But right then, it felt brotherly and compassionate and correct.

And I think it was shortly after that, in those final moments before Headmaster Browning entered the room, that reality hit hard: we were human. The sadness of Jimmy's crash put a chink in our armor. Not only did we care about him, but we had done everything over the years with each other, and there was a consolation in that, knowing we overcame the same struggles. To have someone go down so late was a way of breaking that solidarity, a way of telling us that we were alone going forward, or even worse, that we could drop dead at any given second.

"This one time," sniffled a teary-eyed Alex Mint, "I remember Jimmy and I were at a dance, back in like eighth grade or something, and all you had to do was point to a girl, and Jimmy was on her three seconds later. He'd come back, and he'd know everything about her—her name, her relatives, her birthplace, and her phone number—and a movie date all lined up, every time."

It lightened the mood slightly, brought smiles to peoples' wet faces, and instantly opened up the door for more people to speak, more people who had wanted to say something but held back because we didn't know what was appropriate in these kinds of cases. Over and over, we talked, we listened, and I know I was on the verge of telling the story but just couldn't bring myself to do it because I didn't want to call any more attention to my already weakened emotional state, something my classmates had picked up on already and ribbed me for since I had been acting for some time like the world was going to end.

Junior year, Jimmy and I were hanging out after sports practice because we had a Debate Team meeting that night. He was visibly shaken. Then, for no reason at all, except for that he trusted me as a friend, he confided in me. With that unstable voice you get when you're about to cry, he told me that a girl he really liked, a girl who was his best friend, had died in a car accident just a couple of weeks ago. We'd all heard something about it, but I didn't know just how much it had affected him. He said that if he were to go out, he would want to go out the same way because it just "wasn't fair that she died like that, and I'm still at this big old prestigious school and shit." I didn't know what to say, except that things like this made me question if there was a God or whether the world was even a good place to begin with. I had been dealing with my own quiet teenage depression for a little while at that point, and I had this glum perspective about everything, and hearing Jimmy's story stirred some deep form of compassion within me, this desire to connect with Jimmy in this lonely moment of time where we could. I wanted to put my arm around him, but I couldn't muster the energy. And I'll never forget what he said to me, shaking his head and wiping away a tear in his eye. "No," he started, "No, the world is not a bad place. I think the world is a great place, and the only reason I know that is because we get sad when people die."

Headmaster Browning entered with a flurry, Assistant Headmaster Cork following and Mr. Gittlin right on his trail. He was a wreck. Just like Headmaster Browning earlier, he looked visibly upset. Headmaster Browning now looked hurried and out of breath, and as for Assistant Headmaster Cork, he remained stoic but in a subdued way, as if he had been drugged and was slowly fading away from reality.

"Boys, I appreciate you coming to meet about this very, very sad news. I thought it would be appropriate to speak with you because you are Jimmy's closest friends. I want to fill you in a little more about what is going on, and I hope that we will be able to move along and pray for Jimmy."

He took a deep breath.

"Jimmy had both of his legs amputated. It was necessary; otherwise, he would have died from the horrible damage that was caused when the dashboard drove into his lower knees. He is currently comatose, and the doctors have no idea at the moment what his condition will be, let alone whether he can ever fully regain consciousness. I am hoping that once we're able to cope with this, those of you who wish to see Jimmy will be able to do so in peace. God be on our side."

Pointless to tell you how people received the news. We imagined Jimmy leg-less, without vitality, his athletic body decimated to nothingness, a lonely cripple peddling on the sidewalks, the kind of person we had associated with that group called "the less fortunate" whom we barely knew.

"It is of the utmost importance that you carry on. You *will* be okay. You are the shining light for everyone else. The way you conduct yourself will be noticed by younger students. We will get through this. Just keep faith in Jimmy and in yourselves."

He scanned the room for questions. Or maybe it was just to see how we were feeling.

"You are all dismissed. May God be with you."

After a night of awkward conversation with my parents that involved convincing them I was okay, as well as listening to them on the phone with all the other parents, I returned to school the next day timidly, as if one wrong step could kill my friend. We all acted that way. The fragility of each waking moment became apparent to us; the world moved in slow motion as we became conscious of time and our own mortality. It was no small coincidence that we were reading Wordsworth in senior English during first period, and Mr. Stegman paused on "the still, sad music of humanity" as he looked up from his book and noticed most of us just staring into space or reading the words but not really reading at all. Just that morning, we had received the word in homeroom that Jimmy should hang on for at least a week, which was encouraging news in some ways but also odd in the sense that it placed a timeframe on Jimmy's life. We imagined a clock ticking over his bed now. Before, he could die at any second. But he could also stick around for ten years if he wanted to. Now, his presence felt temporal.

Realizing the fragility of the situation, Mr. Stegman closed his book and sighed.

"You miss Jimmy, don't you, guys?"

We looked at one another, surprised at Mr. Stegman's frankness. He was always kind of rogue. In his early thirties, he was usually setting some stylistic trend: a shirt not fully buttoned, some overly fancy dress shoes, a moppy hairdo. And yet, he had been teaching at the oldest school in North America for almost ten years. We all thought he was a cool guy, but we wondered a little bit about the more personal aspects of his life, which we had to try and decipher through his advisees. Nevertheless, slowly, we responded to him, nodding our heads.

"Yeah, I figured. I miss him, too," and then, pulling a box of cigarettes out of his back pocket as he leaned backward against his desk, "You guys mind?"

We shook our heads; no, of course not, we muttered. Cigarettes, like alcohol, were banned from campus. But it seemed like we were suspending the rules in light of the circumstances, at least for now. Mr. Stegman motioned toward the door. Big Frank Brown went to stand in front of it so that no one could see what Mr. Stegman was doing.

He was kind of spacey, either that or madly intelligent—I couldn't tell which. He propped himself up from the desk and moved over toward the window, which he opened after plopping the cigarettes down on the radiator. There had been a light drizzle, so it was a little dark and damp outside, and we could feel a little wave of coolness entering the room. He sat down on the radiator and lit up a cigarette without hesitation. He took a puff and blew it out the window, looking out at the flagpole and Schoolhouse Field, as if he had forgotten us completely. We sat with anticipation, our senses dulled by Jimmy's condition but magnified by the excitement of some kind of revelation from our teacher.

"Yeah, we all miss Jimmy," he croaked, then a puff, and then, "He's a good kid."

Normally, we'd feel uncomfortable with this bold act of rule-suspending-filibustering. But after all, how many times had Stegman acted like this before? He'd done it countless times, stopping class to talk about discos or crazy nights he had in college. With the top buttons of his shirt loose and the psychedelic designs on it as he kicked back and smoked a cigarette, the hair flowing down to his shoulders, he looked like he had transported himself with a time machine from a 1970s be-in. He was the super friend. Either that, or he was a lonely cowboy, or an old man, or a gas station attendant, someone who had idly watched the years go by and quietly observed all the people that came through over that time. And then, in the same way that Jimmy had confided in me for no reason other than that things just seemed different all of a sudden in his world, Mr. Stegman did the same with us, but more discreetly.

"People are gonna let you down in your life. And you'll never see it coming. They'll build themselves up in you and just ... stomp on you, they'll stomp you out. But Jimmy ... he's not gonna let you guys down. He's gonna go a long way in your lives."

With that, he re-adjusted himself and took a long drag. I didn't quite understand the meaning of Stegman's last line, that Jimmy would go a long way in our lives. What I did silently understand, along with everyone else, was that Stegman was talking about his own personal experience, some tragedy of his, or a set of tragedies, that were far beyond our comprehension, something that would make Jimmy's car accident seem relatively benign by comparison. He rubbed out the cigarette, closed the window, looked at us with a pitying glare, and told us we were dismissed early.

For the rest of the day, we speculated about Stegman's story. An ex-girlfriend? The death of a friend? Or some other kind of accident we couldn't even fathom? A day like that turned into a week like that. The football team lost its opening game 38–0. At halftime, Big Frank Brown ripped into us ("Jimmy would be fucking pissed at you guys!"). The soccer team, suddenly without its captain, looked deflated as well, dropping a 1–0 decision to Filton School. We thought the loss of a friend would inspire us. We didn't realize that it had, but that the sadness had vastly outweighed the inspiration.

During that week, Allen had gone to see Jimmy in the hospital. When he returned to us the next day at school, he was shaken. We, of course, tried to be sensitive to the situation, but we couldn't help but to try and feed our curiosities with questions. What did he look like? Pale, very pale. What had the doctors said? Regained some brain activity. Might make it a while longer. Wasn't that good news? Not the way he looked. Not the way he looked. What do you mean? I can't explain it. Please ... not now. Allen carried himself like that during that whole week. Everything he did was deliberate but without feeling. He was going through the motions. Many of us acted similarly but to a lesser extent. We couldn't help but notice how pale Allen looked. It was as if Jimmy had given him a ghostly kiss of death. We worried about him.

But at the end of the week, Allen's words were confirmed in homeroom by Salim: Jimmy had shown signs of brain activity, and the doctors were hopeful that he might live for weeks, even months. There was a chance he would recover. There was hope. We gave a loud cheer, and Salim introduced a new plan to us: every day after school, or practice, or whatever we had going on, two or three of us would go and visit Jimmy. We'd pick our own groups and sign up on a calendar. Everyone was excited about it, even the ever-stoic Albert Chen, who supported the idea after homeroom in a way that I'd never heard him talk about anything.

The following week, the visits began, and with each passing day, two things happened. First, we received an update on Jimmy. Had he regained brain activity, or had it gone down? We tracked his movements like a banker watching the stock market. The update came at the beginning of every homeroom, and it was followed either by a loud groan or a hearty cheer: time had allowed us a lighter perspective on Jimmy's prognosis even though our hearts were still heavy. Jimmy would have wanted it that way.

The other thing that happened was that two or three boys would come into school each morning with haunted expressions and little to say. Even Big Head Ted looked like he had been raised from the dead. The toll of a sleepless night and reality crashing hard on him had altered his perception of life and his perception of the rest of us as well. He was even apologetic for being a jerk. I just feel terrible about how I talked stuff all the time, he said, I didn't mean it; I was just trying to impress you guys; it was dumb. We told him we didn't know why he was talking about that, and he said never mind. Every day, there was a change for a few of us, and the rest of us just saw the effects. By the time half of us had seen Jimmy, it was as if half of us were in on some big secret, some adult comprehension of seeing the world, and the rest of us were still innocent children.

Eventually, it was time for Denny and me to go visit Jimmy. After wrestling practice, we got in my car and drove over to the hospital. We didn't speak much. We asked each other questions about Jimmy, pointless questions that were about to be answered anyway. What do you think he will look like? Do you think his parents will be there? What should we do when we're there? How long do you want to stay? And then, when that was finished, the usual kind of questions about our upcoming weekend and whatever girls we might be seeing. Appropriately, it was snowing now. Winter had set in, and Jimmy was still alive.

When we got into the hospital room, we didn't know what to focus on first. To the left of the bed were Mr. and Mrs. Chambers, looking just as grief-stricken as we had expected. And then there was Jimmy. He looked like his plain old self, which is what made the whole experience so chilling. It was as if God was mocking us. He was pale, I'll grant Allen that, but it was the complete lifelessness of my friend that moved me. We could see from the shape of the covers that his body was cut off from the hips down, and though we had imagined what that might look like, seeing it in person was jarring, sending a prickly little chill through my own legs.

"Denny, Richie, it's so good to see you guys," Mr. Chambers said softly. "We love seeing all of Jimmy's friends. It means so much to him," Mrs. Chambers added, "so thank you so much. We'll leave you alone."

She smiled at us. An act. An illusion. Mr. Chambers put his hand on her back, faked a smile, and escorted her out of the room. We barely nodded our heads as our attention focused back on Jimmy. We sat on opposite sides of the bed, me to Jimmy's right and Denny to his left. We looked at Jimmy, at each other, at the walls, at nothing at all. We didn't say anything for a long time. We just thought in silence.

At first, when I looked at Jimmy, I was stung with an emotion that I cannot possibly relate to you. I had been gripped by it when I first entered the room but thought it impolite to focus on it too much since his parents were there. Once they left, however, it re-entered my mind. I saw a Jimmy in my mind kicking a soccer ball in a net and then realized what was before me: the lifeless, frail body of a friend who once had everything. I wondered if he would even want to come back to life in this state. I thought of everything he might miss in his life, and I thought of all the people who might miss him in their lives, and then there was this feeling as I looked at the limp blob below me that made me repeatedly gag until I took a few deep breaths, closed my eyes, and assumed my seat. The best way I can describe it is that it was as if some force from Jimmy's crippled body was tugging at me, blurring my thoughts, my vision, my speech, my coherence, and my very own sense of myself.

I thought about my memories of Jimmy again. I hadn't really done this for a couple of weeks. The whole thing had been dragging on, and though we didn't forget Jimmy, the initial sadness we felt had become almost routine. We still felt it, but we weren't as sensitive to it. We had accepted it. It wasn't painfully fresh anymore. And then I wondered if I should feel guilty for not really thinking much about Jimmy until that moment. This was a little routine of mine that had built up over the last year or so in my little bouts of sadness, where I would hate myself for having certain thoughts, or in this case, for not having them. I even realized that thinking of Jimmy more often would have allowed me to feel sorry for myself for a different reason, and I immediately hated myself for having such a selfish thought. The reality was I missed the way I felt sorry for myself. There was something profound about that sadness. I had earned it. And then Denny asked me to leave the room for a few minutes. I was surprised, but I obliged.

I shut the door behind me, and to my surprise, the Chambers family was not there. Perhaps they'd gone to the cafeteria. I thought some more about the stagnancy of the whole Jimmy ordeal. Yes, we were not thinking about him now like we had been when it first happened. We mostly thought about him when we noticed his absence. On Exelauno Day, when several boys recited lines in Latin and Greek in front of the whole school, and a freshman won the big award, we all realized that Jimmy had always declaimed on that day. We remembered him when the wrestling team won by a few points because, with Jimmy, we would have got an update from him about it the next day. We missed him during the debate tournaments at all the big preppy boarding schools in Connecticut because he was a good character to have on the bus. But after a while, when we didn't miss him in those particular instances, life continued as usual. We just had scars.

I eventually wondered what Denny was saying. I debated with myself for a little while, but I just couldn't help but put my ear to the door and listen. "... and you've gotta pull through because, like, for example, Richie's been going through so much, and I don't know what he'll do if you die ..."

I took my ear off the door and narrowed my eyebrows in confusion. What was he talking about? I knew he understood what I'd been going through, but it wasn't like Jimmy and I were best friends. I mean, I was definitely upset about it. And then

I thought, maybe Denny knows me a little better than I really know myself. Maybe this whole thing was weighing on me more than I thought it was. I hadn't cried at all, and Denny knew that, but I think he also saw beyond that: he knew I was hiding my fear. And when Denny said all that stuff to Jimmy, about how he was worried about me, that's when I thought that he was going to be my best friend for life. But strangely enough, I was still kind of pissed at him for making a bold assumption about me and thinking I couldn't handle what was going on.

When he was done, he opened the door, and we stared at each other. It was obvious I had been listening. He hugged me, and I held still. My first thought—in spite of my appreciation for Denny's friendship—was that our classmates would think this was gay if they could see it. But gradually, I came to embrace him harder than I've ever embraced anyone in my family, any girlfriend, or anyone for that matter, and that even includes people at my grandfather's funeral. I told Denny that I didn't want to see Jimmy anymore, and so we left. The doctor had said Jimmy's condition had remained the same, so we gave a neutral report the next day at school.

As time passed, our lives continued to change, but we began to regain the sense of normalcy I had thought about in the hospital. By the new year, we had learned that it was very unlikely that he could ever regain consciousness, which had more or less been assumed already. The issue had become less about life and death and more an ethical issue now of whether or not it would be best to pull the plug on Jimmy's life.

Denny applied and got into Duke early. I was accepted to Dartmouth and became part of that statistic that determined what percent of our class would attend an Ivy League School. That figure was always close to 50%, and if you counted the people like Denny at Duke and the Stanford kids and the MIT kids and so on and so forth, that figure well surpassed 50%. Still, I couldn't help but feel jealous when Denny first got his news, even in spite of my genuine excitement and happiness for him. The feeling, I think, was mutual when, a week later, I called him on the phone with my news. Still, it was a load off our shoulders, and for about half of us, our idea of "school" changed dramatically. The biggest piece of the puzzle was over, and it allowed us to focus on other things.

One of those things was a return to Jimmy. We'd kept up our visits, but slowly, Jimmy had already died within us, and that happened in a tragic way. It was a gradual realization that, even though Jimmy was alive, he was dead. For a few of us, Jimmy was still really alive, and so we never dared to speak about our feelings.

We decided we'd try to encourage Jimmy in any way we could to come back to us. We started decorating his room. We hung up pictures of ourselves on his walls. When we beat Oceanside Academy in the big wrestling meet, Allen took a big photo of the whole team celebrating and pinned it right above Jimmy's bed. Every time I came back, there was some new artistic variation in the room. Allen Craig-Drew, the resident *artiste* of our class, had sculpted a wrestler in a warrior-like pose to commemorate the season Jimmy was missing. It was not Jimmy himself, he said, but a warrior who would fight in Jimmy's place, who would watch over Jimmy as the team battled on.

And battle on they did. Using Jimmy as the catalyst for their motivation and success, they had an undefeated season and won the league championship. Allen, the fearless captain of the team, had reminded them about Jimmy in tearful speeches before every match, and each member of the team won matches that they were not supposed to win. Even though Jimmy's accident had changed the way we moved forward, even though it took us off balance in the way we viewed our schooling and friendship, witnessing our peers use nothing but motivation in the sport of ultimate will and effort and exertion—it replenished us with something that had been missing. Wrestling became the most popular sport that year, and it brought some life back to the school. Our legendary coach, Steve Ward, had been running the program for over thirty years, and he had a way of bringing out the best in each boy by making them a little more loose. He would give out these awards after every match, and one of them was the Terminator award for the fastest pin. After one of the matches, he made an off-color joke that the tree Jimmy crashed into would not win the Terminator award since Jimmy survived the accident, and he gave Jimmy the Guts award after every match for being brave, even though he was not wrestling. Mr. Ward had a double hip replacement, so we would watch him ambling through the hallways with a wry smile on his face, saying, "Jimmy got the Guts again," for no reason whatsoever, his hands out to the side with a slight shrug as he would say it.

As Allen went on to become league champion, New England Champion, and All-American, a magazine caught wind of the story and ran a feature on the school and the friendship between Allen and Jimmy. In it, Allen talked about how using Jimmy as motivation for his success made him feel selfish, but how he still knew Jimmy would be so happy to hear about it when he woke up. When he wakes up, I thought. When he wakes up. I tried to believe.

Soon, and as more of us received our college acceptance letters, we brought this energy to Jimmy in whole new ways. The jazz band performed for him one morning before school, and though we were upset to hear that we would have to miss the jazz band Hall so that they could perform for Jimmy, we felt good knowing that Jimmy would hear it instead. Joey Mazilli asked Allen what they should play, and Allen shrugged his shoulders but said that Jimmy always loved that song "Hang On, Sloopy" and that he wouldn't be surprised if Jimmy found it amusing to play that song over and over again. So that's what the jazz band did, apparently, and with much vigor in doing so as several elderly hospital patients wheeled themselves into the room and clapped their hands, excited to see so many young faces.

We began to paint the walls. At first, the nurse told us not to do it, that the Chambers family would be fined for doing it. We felt dumb. But then Mr. Chambers said, "So what, fine." The nurse shrugged, and after some hesitation and a little goading from Mr. Chambers, the walls gained color. They were red, yellow, brown, crimson, lavender, purple, and even pink. The room was an art exhibit unto itself. It took the place of art class! Mr. Tien took some of his classes there for visits on occasion, mostly his younger kids. For once, it seemed like we were doing something for fun, not just for our college applications. It seemed to give us a sense of meaning. It was a passion. With each stroke of color, with each painted "Get well soon" message, we tried to will Jimmy back to life through some mental force. And the most frustrating part about it was that, in spite of these magnanimous and wide-reaching efforts, every time I looked over at Jimmy for some sign of life, some awakening, he looked more and more dead every time, and we couldn't help but feel that something had been lost.

As winter turned into spring and we began to coast through the rest of senior year, our efforts intensified. We performed plays. We did stand-up comedy routines. We gave play-by-play reports from the baseball team's league championship game, a game that Jimmy would have played in himself. All this on top of what was changing in our personal lives. College decisions, girls, concerts, drugs, alcohol, parties, senior projects—what have you. But we knew to keep our priorities straight. Even though our lives were changing rapidly, Jimmy was our constant. And as we picked up our pace in trying to drag Jimmy back from whatever purgatorial state he was in, we began to connect with each other. We saw, after all, what Stegman may have meant when he said that Jimmy would go a long way in our lives. We bonded over our efforts to bring Jimmy back; we became the closest friends in the world, and we owe that all to Jimmy.

Every boy has a different perspective on how senior year went by at AL. We all saw the tragedy through a different lens.

We all had different histories, different reasons to be sad, different reasons to ask, "Why?" We'd all had different experiences with Jimmy and with each other, and we'd all learned different lessons at different times. But the reason I'm the one of the forty-nine of us telling this story is because of what happened next.

I had been meeting Mr. Stevens regularly throughout the year. I took his words to heart that fateful day when he grabbed me after Headmaster Browning made the announcement about Jimmy. I had spiraled into a deep sadness junior spring when Maria broke up with me and with a series of other events, not the least of which was Jimmy's accident and my grandfather's death. Even though I had not yet cried about Jimmy at all, I felt different. We all did. To me, it was the icing on the cake; my dreary outlook on the world was confirmed by the inexplicable events of a seventeen-year-old boy so full of life suddenly falling asleep at the wheel and crashing into a tree. It seemed altogether unfair to me that his last conscious thoughts were something completely arbitrary as he drove home, that he didn't have time to think beforehand about how much he loved his family and his life. And then I selfishly and nihilistically thought about how I had no such thoughts myself at the time and how maybe I should have assumed Jimmy's place before the accident.

Mr. Stevens was like my own personal, unqualified therapist. Over the course of the year, I had to be referred to a real doctor so that I could obtain a prescription for an antidepressant, but by February, I no longer needed it. It wouldn't be uncommon for us to have some kind of conversation where Mr. Stevens would ask how I was. Was I having any suicidal thoughts? No, none of that, but I guess maybe if something happened to me, I wouldn't mind. Like what? Like if I was in an airplane, and it went down, something like that, but maybe not as violent. So, you're passively suicidal? I guess so. And all of that seemed to relieve Mr. Stevens—it was okay to be passively suicidal, and nevertheless, he'd remind me every time: *you have so much to live for.* And by the end of the year, I was starting to agree as I was prepared to start a new journey at Dartmouth. Now, I was happy it was Jimmy in the hospital bed and not me, and realizing that made me start to hate myself all over again.

I've been holding back on talking about this, but maybe it would make more sense if you understood what happened the year prior. You see, my grandfather was very close to me. He would come to watch every game I played in or any concert I was in, or really anything I was doing. My grandmother had passed away years before, so I guess you could say it gave him something to do. But he very quickly deteriorated, and one day, he fell and broke his hip. He was old and frail, so performing surgery was a major risk, but they were able to do it successfully. My mom went to visit him a few days later and asked if I wanted to come too, but I said no because I had a date with Maria that night and asked if I could come the next day since he was pretty close by. And so, while I was sitting at dinner with Maria later that evening, the waiter came and grabbed me and said there was a phone call for me, and my heart sank. I never forgave myself. And I came to find out that Maria did not have the patience or energy to understand how sad and self-loathing I would become. I should have been there to see him, but I was too preoccupied with less meaningful things and with zero perspective on the fragility of life.

On what seemed like any other day during the last week of the school year, Mr. Stevens came into the student lounge and told me and a few others that we had another emergency hall. The words "emergency hall" rang hollow. We could only assume the worst. As we walked out, Mr. Stevens waited for me as I dragged along and whispered, "I'm glad you're here. Headmaster Browning is looking for you." As he led me to the headmaster's office, I didn't ask any questions. I wondered why Headmaster Browning would need to speak to me in any kind of emergency. I tried to get some clues from Mr. Stevens, but he looked normal, though I couldn't help but feel that he was stealing glances at me here and there, checking to see how I was dealing with this set of consequences or perhaps just reciprocating for my own curiosities. When we finally got to the office, Mr. Stevens knocked, and Headmaster Browning answered the door.

I imagined that what happened next could have occurred in two ways. The first way would be that Headmaster Browning would bring me inside his office, where, much to my surprise, Jimmy would be smiling at me cheerfully from a wheelchair as I would try to avert my gaze from where his legs should be. I'd be surprised that no one had told us about his sudden recovery, a bit confused as to why I was being led into the office, perhaps happy that Jimmy was alive, but above all, jealous. I'd be jealous, I knew, that Jimmy would be elevated to the status of a hero, myself all the more saddened that perhaps I would lose the solidarity I had built all year with my classmates rallying around his soon-to-be-corpse, angry that his stubborn, selfish refusal to *just die already* had put such terrible thoughts into my head in the first place.

But when Headmaster Browning ushered me inside the empty room, I realized that my second guess of events was more accurate, and I knew well before he told me that Jimmy had died. It simply wouldn't have made sense for me to be there and not Allen if Jimmy had lived. Immediately, I was relieved, as if some kind of burden had been lifted off my back, and what followed was a terrifying wave of guilt for my relief, which replaced the burden altogether. It was in those few seconds that I finally realized what Jimmy had meant to me. I wanted to magically reproduce him so I could tell him I was sorry for my rash thoughts about his selfishness and my jealousy that he would be a hero. In those painstakingly long few seconds of inner turmoil, I realized that I didn't like myself too much—maybe hated myself—for these kinds of morbid thoughts I had and that I wanted someone like Jimmy around to prove to myself that I could do without those thoughts, and, finally, because I truly did miss him and hadn't really known it all along.

I'd never felt so conflicted in my life when he told me that Jimmy had passed away that afternoon. It's a hazy recollection, but pretty much Headmaster Browning waved me in and invited me to take a seat. I put my hands on my lap and leaned forward as he assumed the seat in front of me. I was calmer and more anxious, perhaps, than I had ever been in my life. He took a deep breath and looked me in the eyes.

"Richie, I'm very sorry to tell you this, but aside from Allen, you are really the first to find out that Jimmy has passed away this afternoon. The doctors have known for some time now that Jimmy would never regain consciousness. Even if he did by some faint miracle, he would be a shell of his former self, and the Chambers family couldn't bear to let Jimmy continue suffering. They wanted him to move on."

He offered me a tissue. I declined. Something sad was stirring inside me. I had already grieved for Jimmy some time ago, for the whole year really, and in some ways, he had already died many times. At the same time, his corporeal presence, the thought in my mind that I knew his body was out there in that hospital, gave me a sense of comfort that he was still alive, that there was some kind of hope, however slight. And then, after that, I asked myself in anger why Jimmy's parents would pull the plug on that chance. Yes, to redeem myself for my morbid thoughts, I forced myself to hate Mr. and Mrs. Chambers. I sat there angrily, narrowing my eyebrows at Headmaster Browning, trying my best to maintain my disappointment in them. But slowly, during that short silence, I knew I was probably being rash, that I couldn't repent for my evil thoughts just by having more of them. Hell, the Chambers family had so much money, it was not an issue of resources: they couldn't bear the deterioration of their son as he lay legless, unconscious in a hospital bed each passing day, torturing all of his family and friends with a hope that would never come to fruition.

After that, I discovered why Headmaster Browning needed to see me. He put his hand over mine on the coffee table in front of us. The contact took me aback.

"Richie, I know you've been very, very sad at times, and you were doing a lot better, but I'm worried about you now."

I was seething. I thought I had built a trust with Mr. Stevens, but he had backstabbed me and told my deepest secrets to Headmaster Browning. I continued to be mad at Mr. Stevens until the end of that day, when I finally realized (gratefully) that Mr. Stevens hadn't betrayed me at all but had instead tried to help me. Yet, in that moment, I angrily brushed aside any notion that I was sad.

"Richie, I've called you in here because I'm worried about everyone. I'm worried about Allen. I'm worried about you. I don't know how they'll take this. You're an immensely well-respected figure in this community. You've also been through something like this before. I need to know a few things."

I nodded.

"Will you be okay?"

I nodded again, more assertively.

"Can you help everyone else to be okay? They really look up to you. That's why you're here. You know how to fight."

"Yes, of course," I said without hesitation.

"Good," Headmaster Browning said. And then, unexpectedly, he began crying. I didn't know what to do. I always felt subservient to the faculty. I felt like I'd cry before they would in all situations. Here I was with a grown man, an established religious figure used to caring for others, crying before me.

"My last question is that I worry about everyone; I worry about you handling this. It would break my heart if any of you did not see the light in the world. You all forget how lucky you are sometimes. Please promise me you will all be okay."

I thought of the time Jimmy told me about his friend in the car accident and how I had an outpouring of faith in him in that single moment of time, how I wanted so desperately to let him know that I was exactly the same person he was. The reason I tell you all this, it's because that's how I felt about Headmaster Browning then, and I let him know as much.

"We will all be okay," I declared on behalf of my 48 peers. "I promise."

Headmaster Browning and I were the last people to enter the hall. I took the empty seat next to Allen, who was, surprisingly, not in tears. Perhaps he felt the same way about having grieved for some time already. Maybe he was trying to be strong in front of everyone else. Either way, when I got there, we looked at each other and nodded our heads in silent understanding, and I saw a sadness in his eyes that almost brought me to tears for the first time in a long time. The school was quieter than it had ever been when Headmaster Browning got to the podium, ironically quieter at full capacity than at any moment when it was empty. I imagined the stillness of the place, the desolation, the nothingness. I imagined the empty playing fields that knew so much about victory and defeat. I imagined the empty halls that knew only of the stories it had overheard us telling about what we were learning in school and in life. I imagined the darkened classrooms that knew us as friends. And that's when the school breathed new life into me, when I realized that the school was not a place but a being, a thing that desperately wanted to mold us into young men but could never really know us at all. It had seen so much, and it was grieving for us now, in silence.

"It is with great sadness," Headmaster Browning choked out, "that I have to tell you that Jimmy Chambers has died."

The reaction was mixed at first. For most of us, our fears were confirmed: this was the end of our futile battle, the one we'd waged some time ago, knowing full well that we'd lose. Some gasped, others remained calm. But Headmaster Browning paused because he didn't know what to do next, and that's when it happened. Allen stood up next to me and just started clapping. You'd think it was completely inappropriate, but it felt like the most appropriate and correct thing to do in my life when I got up next to him and clapped frantically. I clapped until my hands hurt. Soon, all of the other seniors were standing. And then the juniors, and the sophomores, until the sixies and the faculty, and even Headmaster Browning all followed our example. We clapped for what seemed like minutes on end, but I have to guess that it was really a minute ovation for Jimmy. We clapped to celebrate his life. And when it was over, and Headmaster Browning explained exactly what had happened and when the funeral would be, we had no regrets.

We graduated a few days later. It was the last time we sang "Jerusalem" together, which was my favorite song in all of our halls. I remember Denny turning to me and raising his arms as if he had an imaginary bow and arrow when we reached the line "Bring me my bow / of burning gold" and the way all the seniors yelled the "O!" before "clouds unfold."

Mr. Stevens was also there, as were all of the faculty members, and I thanked him for his sincere attempts to help me through the years, and in confidence, I told him that I was okay, that I was ready for a change, that I'd stay in touch, and that we'd grab a beer the moment I turned 21. He told me to fuck that because we were going to get one the moment I graduated that day. I smiled, and I realized I was getting older, and it actually made me sad. It might seem like graduation would be a fitting end to my senior year, but that was not the case at all.

By some cruel twist of fate, Jimmy's funeral was the following morning. Although we all could have met at the Church, we decided to meet at the school and take a bus over together. Even though we had dressed up in a jacket and tie for graduation the day before, it was an odd sight to see everyone in that attire with their dull expressions. Jacket and tie events were supposed to be happy ones, like graduation. And now, there was no room for happiness.

We boarded the bus and rode in silence. I sat next to Denny, and though I'd realized that the end had come to our AL days, I knew our friendship would last forever. We knew at that time, though, that it wasn't the right time to discuss such things, and so I rode with my head against the window wet with rain.

While the priest was talking, I tried to think about the whole year and what it would mean for me going forward. By now, I had learned to consider how it would affect us, not just me. In fact, I thought to myself, that is what mattered the most. Yes, I realized, this might be the last time all of us will be together until our five-year reunion. I looked around at everyone without trying to draw too much attention to myself, and then I looked down at the pit with the casket below me, and I tried to figure out what exactly we had learned. When I came up with an answer, I began to cry for the first time since we had heard the news about Jimmy back in the fall, but it wasn't because I was completely sad over the realization.

We learned that Wordsworth was not full of it when he wrote about his pending mortality. We learned that you could find out more about someone over a cigarette than a piece of chalk. We learned that sometimes you learn who your best friends are behind closed doors. We learned how lucky we were, but that we were undeniably human. Above all—as the 49 of us tossed our diplomas into Jimmy's earthy grave—we learned that love was never fleeting.

ACKNOWLEDGMENTS　　—

Within every individual, there is a creative spirit. I am grateful that my parents let mine shine through. They are both lawyers, and I cannot think of a single time when they encouraged me to be the same. They just wanted me to be the best version of myself. I am forever grateful for their love and support.

I also draw inspiration from my older brother, James, who is the real author in the family. It was not easy growing up in his shadow, and he pushed me to pursue my own ambitions.

I also want to thank my wife, Julianne, who always supports me in everything that I decide to pursue.

Of course, I am indebted to the countless teachers at Roxbury Latin and Princeton who helped in my development as a writer, as well as all of the students who peer-reviewed my work along the way. A special gratitude goes to Edmund White, my thesis advisor at Princeton, who helped me develop these stories many years ago.

I also want to acknowledge Steven Leshinger, who was a partner in crime in helping me edit these stories over the last couple years.

Lastly, I want to thank you for deciding to read these stories. I hope that they make their intended impact.

ABOUT ATMOSPHERE PRESS —

Founded in 2015, Atmosphere Press was built on the principles of Honesty, Transparency, Professionalism, Kindness, and Making Your Book Awesome. As an ethical and author-friendly hybrid press, we stay true to that founding mission today.

If you're a reader, enter our giveaway for a free book here:

SCAN TO ENTER
BOOK GIVEAWAY

If you're a writer, submit your manuscript for consideration here:

SCAN TO SUBMIT
MANUSCRIPT

And always feel free to visit Atmosphere Press and our authors online at atmospherepress.com. See you there soon!

ABOUT THE AUTHOR   —

JEFF KIRCHICK is the author of *How Boys Learn*, which is his second publication. His first book, *Authentic Selling: How to Use the Principles of Sales in Everyday Life*, was a winner of the Independent Press Award. Jeff majored in English with Certificates in Creative Writing and French at Princeton University, and this collection of short stories is adapted from his senior thesis of the same title, written under the tutelage of Edmund White.

Jeff's career to date has been focused in technology sales, and he was previously a sales leader for a startup that he led to a successful exit in 2021. Though he continues to work in tech sales, he has ambitions to become an author/screenwriter.